InstaBook

An Ace in Masquerade

A novel of love, deception, and valor

by James Winnefeld

To a friend, classmate, bon vivant, and fellow author, with warm regard

Jim Winnefeld

Denlinger's Publishers, Ltd.
P.O. Box 1030
Edgewater, Florida 32132

Library of Congress Cataloging-in Publication Data
ISBN: 0-87714-603-9

This is a work of fiction. All characters and events portrayed in this book are fictional, and any resemblance to real people or incidents is purely coincidental.

Forward

During World War II the Navy expanded from a total personnel strength of 200,000 in 1940 to some 5,000,000 in 1945. It is one of life's minor miracles that the Navy was able to keep track of all -- or nearly all -- of these millions of officers and sailors during a time of such great expansion and the millions of transfers of personnel from one duty station to another. The Navy personnel system had the obligation to order its sailors to and from training and to and from shore stations, ships, and squadrons, to see that they were paid, to look after their health and welfare, and to know where all were at any given moment. The Navy's personnel procedures -- and customs -- served it well during this hectic and often chaotic period. But this novel centers on a case where the process broke down and one officer with some connivance was able to assume the identity of another.

To readers unfamiliar with the tremendous turnover and movement of personnel during the War the scenario that is described on these pages will appear incredible. There were -- and are -- too many checks and balances that serve to insure a person is who he says he is. But those who experienced the "fog of war" (not all of which occurred on the battlefield) will find believable most of the story that is told.

Too often forgotten is the fact that World War II was fought largely by teenagers, or young men just out of their teens. Most of the Navy's pilots were in their very early twenties and some were in fact in their late teens.

One need only recall former President George Bush's experience of becoming a naval aviator at the age of 19. These young men made mistakes in combat and in judgments in dealing with the Navy's system of organizing for combat. The protagonist in this story is such an individual. Placed at the interface between the Navy's peacetime system for managing its officer corps and the exigencies of a brutal war, he exploits the gaps for his personal survival. While his conduct is often not admirable, he somehow manages to serve his country and his Navy well. In sum, this novel is a story of human weakness and strength in the face of adversity and of courage in coping with the challenges of the chaos of war.

Chapter 1 - Augering In

It was all a terrible mistake. In the one and half seconds left in John Deal's short life he realized he had screwed up. His F-6F Hellcat was powering down at 365 knots-- much too fast -- in a forty degree dive as he neared the end of his practice strafing run. His six guns were firing at the rocky target, raising a column of dust from the hits and numerous splashes from the misses as the 50 caliber bullets struck the water beyond the rocks. But the target rapidly grew too large in his gunsight and he frantically pulled back on the stick. But to his horror it became obvious that the plane's nose was not going to rise enough to get him clear of the target. In the brief interval between realization and impact John Deal screamed out over his open radio: "Damn, damn, da......"He didn't have time to say more because his neck was broken instantly as his head snapped forward on impact and the cockpit control panel smashed into his chest. A fireball fed by spewing aviation gasoline completed the triumph of aerodynamics over stupidity and conceit. John Deal had never been as good a pilot as he thought he was. Now he would never have the time to close the gap between the wish and the fact.

On that sunny, nearly cloudless Hawaiian morning in late spring, John Deal's wingman, "Acey" Dusey, saw it all unfold since he was the number two in the string of planes diving on the target. Acey had shouted "pull up, pull up" just before Deal's hellcat hit just beyond the target and disintegrated. But not only was the warning too late, it was never transmitted at all because Acey in his horror had forgotten to key his mike. Pulling up into a wingover he was appalled by how fast it had happened and how final it was. There one minute and dog meat the next. The other aircraft in his flight pulling up to circle over the target had already started to chatter on the radio." Did you see that fucker hit?"

"Holy Christ, he just augered in."

"There ain't enough left to pick up with a foxtail and dustpan. Shit, Johnny was supposed to leave tomorrow to get in the war." These obscenities and mouthings of the obvious continued until the flight leader broke in and shouted over his radio: "Shut the fuck up you bastards and let me get a call in to base to send out a recovery party."

As the five remaining Hellcats joined up to return to the Lahaina Naval Air Station, all that was left of John Deal's life were scattered bits of metal and viscera topped by a column of black smoke that soon rose to fifteen thousand feet over Kahoolawe target and flattened out in an anvil shaped cloud as the upper winds took hold of the smoke plume. That afternoon the recovery party found only enough bits and pieces of aircraft and pilot to fill a small packing case. The disgusted petty officer in charge spat out John Deal's epitaph: "Why couldn't the fucker have hit the water a hundred yards beyond the rocks and saved us the trouble. Fuckin aviators fly, drink, and screw and leave us to clean up their mess."

John Deal had taken off from Lahaina Naval Air Station that morning on his final flight. So let us take a closer look at the new air station on the gentle rise behind

Lahaina City. Carved out of the red lava soil the air station had taken up some of the best pineapple plantation land on the beautiful Island of Maui. It was a busy place. Its mission was to hone the skills of a pool of aviators who would in good time be sent forward to replace pilots lost in combat. Some pilots were there only a week, others two months or more, before being sent to the South Pacific or to the Navy's growing number of carriers gathering in the Central Pacific. In the minds of naval aviation's personnel pipeline planners the Lahaina Naval Air Station was little more than a "holding tank" in which to stockpile aviators intended to fill gaps in the fleet, gaps that would surely develop as the new carriers took the war to the Japanese empire in the central Pacific in the coming summer. In the late spring and early summer of 1943 NAS Lahaina was populated by brand new F-6F Hellcats and F-4U Corsairs, piloted for the most part by brand new Navy and Marine pilots ("nuggets" because the gold on their Navy wings was so new). But the new planes were in better condition than the pilots. Replacement pilots at Lahaina were not an elite breed. Rather, they were the leftovers, the fuckups, the slow learners, and the square pegs that for good reason had not been assigned directly to the newly formed carrier squadrons. They considered themselves second class citizens, cannon fodder, and "misunderstood" by a Navy that was led by Annapolis "ring knockers" who in the opinion of the replacement pilots saw the war mainly as a career opportunity.

The leaders of this irritable and irritating group of misfits were themselves second stringers who had been "sent home" as a result of combat fatigue, because they had spent too much time at the bar, or were the result of the inevitable screwups as the wartime Navy collided with the traditions and regulations of the peacetime navy. The leaders were mostly lieutenant commanders who would never make commander. One of the two full commanders in the group was Jake Womble who was the skipper of replacement Fighter Squadron 321.

Jake Womble was too senior for this job. But Jake was an alcoholic and the Navy needed all the experience -- drunk or sober -- it could get in commanding officer positions. Jake's assignment officer justified sending him to the job because "Even Jake can't screw this one up."

The attack on Pearl Harbor had saved Jake from a letter of caution, a career killer in the peacetime Navy, and sent him to a fighter squadron on the Lexington. But the bottle licked him there just as it had as a staff officer in Pensacola. On this hot, humid, and windless afternoon Jake sat behind his desk in the Butler hut that served as the "head shed" for his squadron. A tall gaunt man with a perpetually pissed off expression on his sallow countenance, he pondered how to spend the rest of the morning. At the moment he craved a drink and his hands shook slightly as he tapped an unlighted cigarette against his wrist for the third time. He had tapped so hard that the cigarette had bent double and he threw it disgustedly into the nearby waste basket. Jake Womble had two problems. First, he had just lost another F-6 in a stupid accident. The second case of target fixation this week. What the hell was the training command teaching these clowns? He was getting nasty messages from his boss at Ford Island over in Pearl Harbor wanting to know why his accident rate was so bad. Jake mumbled barely audibly, "Bastard's in a cushy billet close to the Admiral, spending his weekends on the cocktail circuit in Honolulu and fucking nurses in his spare time. Spends his work day sending snotty messages to the people doing the dirty work."

But Jake Womble's second problem was more troubling than the questions asked by "those pussies back at Pearl Harbor." He was looking at the record of a summary court martial of one of his charges. Ensign Jack Dell had helped wreck a bar in Lahaina, been a passenger in a jeep involved in a hit and run accident, and had slugged a shore patrolman so hard that the injured "SP" had to be air evacked to Trippler Army Hospital on Oahu to be put back together. The Court had thrown the book at young Jack Dell -- loss of pay, restriction to quarters, a suspended brig sentence, and a recommendation that he be returned to the enlisted ranks. Any less a sentence and Jake would have had the civil authorities and the admiral on his neck. No question that Dell had to be sent home where he would probably be busted and serve out the rest of his war in the ranks as a "white hat."

As Jake reflected on Dell's escapades, he thought, "What a waste this goddam war is. We kill our enemies, ruin good men, and piss away airplanes, equipment, and dollars. Meanwhile our women are back in the states wanting to get laid, booze is waiting to get drunk, and factory workers are getting overtime pay." As he thought this over -- particularly the part about the waiting women he gently hefted the slight weight of Jack Dell's slim service record. "What about this hell-raiser Jack Dell?" Jake thumbed through his record. A widower father in Oregon, no sisters or brothers, not married. Two years at the University of Oregon before joining up after Pearl Harbor. A loner, but a kid who apparently flew well. Highest flight grades in training he had ever seen in this bunch of fuckups and shakey throttle jockeys. Womble shook his head and muttered, "Well, he must have screwed up somewhere or I wouldn't have gotten him. Christ, he had only been in this squadron for a week when he went haywire." He couldn't even recall having met him. But then he hadn't met that kid John Deal either. And now one of these screwups had gone up in smoke and the other was getting shipped home to face a crummy future.

The Court Martial had been convened and done its work quickly. They didn't screw around. "Had to send a message to these guys that they are naval officers, not a bunch of truck drivers and stevedores." Jake sighed as he put Jack Dell's service record aside and signed the record of the court martial thus approving the sentence adjudged. He wondered what action the Admiral's judge advocate would recommend as he took final action on the record. But Jake saw one more piece of paper to look at before he put Jack Dell out of his life and went to an early lunch -- and a few beers -- at the "O" Club. It was Dell's orders back to the States for further disposition and assignment. He wondered what Pensacola would do with this guy. He quickly scratched his signature on the orders.

Licking his lips Jake Womble shouted out through

the swinging doors that served as the entrance to his office. "Putty, get your ass in here. I am through with this Dell kid. Let's get him out of here"

Yeoman Chief Petty Officer Elmo "Putty" Benson shambled into the office. A large fleshy red faced man with a beaked nose and little hair on his head, he was sweating profusely and carried a look of annoyance that was so deeply etched into his face that he must have been complaining all his life. He had all the appearances of a heart attack waiting to happen. He took the folders from Jake Womble, glanced at them to insure they were signed ("Got to hold these fuckin' officers' hands even while they pee"), and then rasped out.

"He's gone. But I gotta have somebody to inventory Ensign Deal's personal effects. And who are we going to send in his place to VF-241? I got another phone call from a buddy in AirPac this morning bitching about how slow we are in getting these guys out of here. He said unless we speed things up, you are going to get a rocket from the Admiral."

"Christ, Putty, get the XO to take care of all that stuff. I'm busy as hell."

"Sir, remember? The XO left for Pearl last night and won't be back for a week. I'll get somebody to inventory Deal's stuff and look around for someone to take his place while you have lunch ("I won't see the fucker for the rest of the day. Just as well. I can run this place drunk better than he can sober.").

As Womble waved him out of the office and headed for the door himself, Chief Benson picked up the phone and called "Boy's Town," the set of junior aviator dormitory Quonset huts. A sleepy sailor answered the phone and Benson barked:

"Tell Dell to get his sweet ass up here to the squadron office to pick up his orders back to the States."

Slamming the phone down, he thought: "Here we are sending a guy back to the States and I've got to find a warm body to send to VF-241. There's got to be an easier way."

As he mouthed the words, the germ of a fantasy began to form in his mind. A chief petty officer of the peacetime Navy, Putty Benson's fantasy was to play God without his seniors noticing it. Sort of like the stewards who were the officers' cooks and servants. The scuttlebutt was that when the officers got them riled up, they just pissed in the officers soup before it was served in the wardroom. He had heard that some officers had even told the chief steward that they had never had soup that tasted so good. "Serve the buggars right. Now what can we do here -- today -- to square this fucking birdfarm away?" Putty Benson's slick mind began to pick up speed as he considered the options......

Chapter 2 - Scam

He was in his skivvy shorts and lying on his bunk looking at the ceiling of the Quonset hut that he shared with a dozen other replacement pilots. He seemed to be just above average height, though it was difficult to tell for sure until he swung his legs over the side of his bunk and rested his head on his knees. When he looked up it was apparent that his body was wiry rather than compact. There was nothing awkward about his movement as he reached for the pack of cigarettes and lighter lying on the packing crate that served as a night stand. As he looked up at the old schoolroom clock dangling from a wire attached to the bulkhead, a fuller appraisal of Jack Dell could be made. Such an appraisal would take in his short dark hair, a long almost straight nose that had been banged up and then imperfectly straightened sometime in his past, and penetrating dark eyes that suggested he was not a person to trifle with. He gave the impression of tightly coiled energy -- looking for a place to unwind -- and impatience that was bottled up only by an extreme effort. He flexed and unflexed his muscles as he lit the cigarette that appeared to be screwed into his mouth. He was sweating profusely. Ensign Jack Dell was thinking over the events of the past week.

"Shit, when will I learn to leave the juice alone? If I don't watch it, I'm gonna be a boozer just like my old man. What a fucking mess! Tearing down Shorty Kaanui's bar coulda been smoothed over and the bill paid. I wasn't driving the jeep when it hit that poor Hawaiian kid who didn't move fast enough. But dammit all to hell, I was the guy who had to beat the shit out of that shore patrolman -- pounded him so hard I don't even remember being pulled off." With that thought He reached for his head, messaged an obvious bump, and then winced and groaned. "When will I learn that fists can't fill in for smarts? Just like that dustup in Corpus when I creamed that fucking wise-ass at the club bar. How was I to know he was a Marine major? His flight suit was the same as mine. I was lucky to get out of that one alive. I probably still have marines looking for my ass back there."

"I've gotta start thinking insteada hittin'. Next time a wise-ass gets me riled, I've gotta learn to stuff it, eat shit, and smile at the bastard rather than decking him."

"But being smart sure as hell didn't save that guy this morning -- plowing a furrow in Kahoolawe rocks. He lost control of himself and bought the farm. I lost the handle and am being sent back gift wrapped for screwing for the rest of the war. If only there was a way out of this mess. I'd lie, cheat, or steal to have the orders that kid had until this morning. He didn't know how good he had it until it was too late. I wonder what kind of a guy he was. Was he like me? Hell, I don't think I remember ever seeing him. Can't have been here more than 10 days. As bad as things are I would rather be me than him. I wonder if I can talk my way out of this: 'Geez sir, I didn't know what I was doing. All I want to do is kill Japs. Take my pay, bust me, but don't ground me and don't send me back before I show what I can do... Shit, the godawful truth is that I've never been any good at sweet talking except when the target was a piece of ass. I can't even keep my fuckin' mouth shut when I need to. Pa was right. It was my acting up that killed Ma and forced me to get out of town ahead of that candy-assed sheriff. Somehow, I gotta get my stuff together -- like I do when I strap on an airplane....."

At that moment in his reverie Jack Dell was startled by a clanging against the side of the hut just above his head. Snooper McGee, the sailor detailed to clean the officers' huts, shouted above the din: "Mr. Dell, Chief Benson says the skipper wants to see you NOW.

He said to get your ass moving-- SIR."

Jack started to get up and snarled, "A little more respect, McGee, or I'll hang you by the balls on the clothesline. In the meantime get out of my sight before I hurt you. I ain't got a thing to lose if I bust you up a bit!"

"There I go again," Jack mumbled, "Fists instead of smarts. Will I ever get it right? I swear I'm going to keep my mouth shut when I see that lard butt chief."

Fifteen minutes later Jack Dell reported at the squadron office hut. He looked better than he felt as he muttered to Chief Benson. "Reporting to the skipper as ordered."

Benson looked Dell up and down and then said, "Shit, you just missed him. I have your orders and your copy of your court martial papers here. You can sign for them now or wait until the skipper comes back -- but damned if I know when that will be. While you think on that he has a chore for you. He ordered that you inventory and pack Ensign Deal's personal effects -- he's the guy who tried to blow up the target this morning over at Kahoolawe -- and get them back up here this afternoon. You can stop by base supply for packing boxes. Any questions? No? Here are the inventory forms, and now sir if you'll excuse me I'll get back to work."

Benson added quickly, "If you hurry I've got you a standby slot on the Gooney Bird flight over to Ford Island at 1700."

Jack nodded at these instructions and thought, "This is the first of a lifetime of shitty details coming my way. No point is pissing off this old windbag. Time to get on with it."

As he returned to the officers' huts he felt a small stirring of pride that he hadn't mouthed off to the old chief (What the hell good would it have done?) or taken his guff with a chip on his shoulder.

After a greasy hamburger and a cup of Kool-aid in the officers' mess, Jack turned to starting an inventory of John Deal's personal effects. He emptied the contents of Deal's stand up metal locker onto his bunk and kicked out the foot locker from beneath it. He also emptied the contents of a sea bag hanging beside the locker. He was not surprised to see a half full bottle of Old Granddad come flying out of the bottom of the seabag. As he surveyed the pile of personal belongings on Deal's mattress cover ("fart sack"), he groaned: "What a bunch of crap this guy collected!" Uniforms of every description including dress blues that no sailor west of San Francisco would ever need. A pile of letters with rubber bands around them, a wallet ($32 in cash -- "No point in pocketing that. The fucker was bound to have some money. Chief will want to know how much there was."), a carton of Luckies (these quickly put aside for Jack's personal use), two packs of rubbers ("His family won't need them" as he tossed them in the trash can), several snapshots of his various girlfriends ("The guy had a good eye for a piece of ass.") and an elderly woman ("Probably his mom."), and a set of official documents including his orders to VF-241 ("When ordered, detach from Replacement Fighter Squadron Three Two One, NAS Lahaina, T.H., and report without delay to the nearest Navy port of embarkation and proceed as directed by competent authority to Fighter Squadron Two Four One wherever it may be located....Upon arrival report to Commanding Officer for duty involving operational and training flights.").

He reviewed the orders carefully. The detaching endorsement was already filled out, signed, and dated with today's date. As far as the Navy was concerned, John Deal was already outta here. ("One minor detail: he went out feet first!") Jack Dell gradually realized he was holding in his hand a loaded gun in the form of orders just waiting to be carried out by John Deal -- or by whoever wanted to be John Deal for a while. Except for last minute packing Deal had been ready to detach and haul ass as soon as he got back from the flight he never finished this morning.

Attached to his orders was John Deal's service record. He had been born, raised, and schooled in Canoga Park, California. Jack noted that while his parents were still living, they were not identified as next of kin on his "If I should die..." sheet. "Strange to list a great aunt but not his parents as next of kin -- unless they had had a falling out." Deal had spent a year at UCLA before signing up for the Navy flight program right after Pearl Harbor. Jack snorted, "Another fuckup like me looking for a way out of college and a little excitement. Well, apparently no one will miss him except his great aunt. Be interesting to see how the skipper writes a condolence letter to a great aunt!"

Jack quickly and less than carefully inventoried and packed the effects and then filled out the inventory lists. He held out Deal's orders, service record, flight log, and his photos and bundles of letters. His curiosity was aroused by the fact that Deal had some sort of problem with his parents since there were no letters from them in the packets of letters. He looked at the slimmest bundle of letters. There were three letters from a lady who clearly must have been the great aunt listed as next of kin. The letters expressed pride in Deal's accomplishments in the Navy and one of them made a plea for him to end his quarrel with his parents before he went into combat. The cause of that estrangement was not clear but the context was that it had occurred while Deal was in college. Apparently no correspondence had been exchanged with his parents since he had entered the Navy in January 1942, a year and half ago.

The other letters were from a large number of girl friends. The content was extremely explicit and erotic. John Deal had been a cocksman of the first order and must have carried on a very interesting correspondence. Jack wished that he could see the letters that Deal had written to ignite and encourage such passion. One set of three letters were particularly interesting. This writer had apparently attended UCLA with Deal and clearly was deeply in love with him. The letters were more tender than erotic. They referred to a memorable evening a month or so earlier -- just before Deal left for Hawaii. This girl -- a lovely round hand -- was Margaret Fitzgibbons. Her letters were signed "Maggie." The return address indicated she lived in Palos Verdes Estates overlooking L.A.. She apparently had a war job, but still lived with her parents. A snapshot enclosed in one of the letters showed a lovely slim girl with blond hair, a high forehead, and memorable eyes. Quite a knockout. A college beauty queen? She was clearly in the class of a large group of women who by the evidence must have had big tits and pea brains. It didn't seem to matter to Deal: he had apparently screwed them all with abandon. If his mind hadn't been so much on screwing and been more on flying, he might have enjoyed each for a few years more of both.

The last pack of three letters was from some guy Deal's age in San Francisco. And it quickly became apparent that Deal's sexual interests were not discriminating. From all indications he was apparently a bisexual who enjoyed playing a very wide field indeed. "A fucking queer who sucked Deal's cock. In the meantime Deal is screwing every bitch on the west coast. A real hero. What a loss to his clientele -- but no loss to the Navy."

Jack closed up the packing boxes and then packed his own belongings before heading back to the squadron office. Chief Benson was sitting at his desk while a yeoman petty officer was typing rapidly at a dilapidated desk in the corner of the hut.

Benson looked up as Jack entered and said, "Skipper's still not back yet. I don't think we will see him until tomorrow morning, but things are fixed up so that you can go and catch that plane this afternoon if a slot opens up."

Benson then turned to his yeoman and said, "Beat it, Whitey, I got to have some words with Mr. Dell. Come back in an hour."

Benson then asked, more politely than was his want, that Jack take a chair. And then he started to talk -- facing away from Jack and intermittently turning and looking at the wall over Jack's shoulder.

"Mr. Dell, I have to shovel a lot of shit through here in one day. The skipper is too busy (this with a smirk) to take care of a lot of it. Right now I am faced with the following. Getting you to sign your record of court martial and either accepting or refusing (Benson lifted his eyes at this) your right of appeal to the findings and sentence of the court as approved by the convening authority. Next, I gotta be creative and put the skipper's signature on your orders out of here. Let me tell you that tomorrow he won't know whether he signed them or not. Next, I got to countersign on behalf of the skipper your inventory of Mr. Deal's personal effects. Next, I have got to get those personal effects over to base supply for shipping. Next, I have got to get two messages over to base communications: the first tells the Bureau of Fucking Naval Personnel that Mr. Deal doesn't live here -- or anywhere else -- anymore. The second is a telegram to Mr. Deal's next of kin telling them that the U.S. of A. regrets to inform them that their beloved son, nephew, or whatever was killed in a stupid-assed accident. And finally, I have to find someone in this fucked up squadron to take Mr. Deal's place in VF-241 out in the stinking swamps somewhere in the Solomons. That won't be easy because none of these peckerheads wants to go to the jungle -- they came to fly off a birdfarm where the air is cleaner and the Japs ain't as thick as fleas."

With this last Chief Benson turned and looked Jack straight in the eyes. "Mr. Dell, you can help me with a lot of this, starting with waiving your right of appeal to your court martial so I don't have to go through a lot of useless paperwork -- that in the end won't make a snail's fart worth of difference either way. I am also going to ask you politely to take Mr. Deal's personal effects and drop them off over at Base Supply on your way to the air terminal to catch your plane in an hour. I am also going to ask you to drop off these two messages at base communications, letting the world know that John Deal no longer exists. If you will do these things, I will see that you have maximum elbow room for whatever you want to make out of your future. Do we understand one another?"

Jack Dell caught the drift of the Chief's meaning down to the last sly hint. He could do what he wanted with John Deal, his gear, and his papers so long as he kept Chief Benson out of it. It took him just a split second to answer.

"Chief, I will waive my appeal rights. You just get those papers signed, leave the rest to me, and I will do the right thing. I assume the skipper's usual follow up letter to Deal's next of kin and the redirecting of his mail will receive proper consideration? And that the copy of my orders that is usually sent to my next duty station will also receive proper consideration?"

As Jack said these words, he saw Chief Benson write three ticks on the paper in front of him -- while Benson was thinking, "This kid didn't lose a beat." Benson looked up and his eyes bore into Jack. "Mr. Dell we never had this conversation. I got my ass covered and yours is hanging out if there is any comeback."

As Benson signed the papers, Jack said, "Chief, under the circumstances it has been a pleasure. I will buy you a drink in Tokyo."

With that, Jack went out the door, told the driver of his jeep to get out, that he had some errands to run, and to pick up the jeep at base operations in 30 minutes. In thirty minutes Jack had visited the disbursing office (signing papers to get all of Jack Dell's future pay sent by allotment to his checking account at a bank in Eugene, Oregon), Base Supply (to forward his own personnel effects to NAS Pensacola for pickup at a later date), base communications (to say goodbye to the attractive WAVE on duty), and the base dump (to say goodbye to John Deal's personal effects). He then proceeded to base operations and entered the crude passenger lounge in the terminal hut. He identified himself as Ensign Jack Dell and was told he was logged in as a standby on the flight due to leave in 20 minutes. In response he was told by the terminal petty officer that there was an Ensign John Deal ahead of him -- who for some reason had not shown up yet. Five minutes before the doors of the old "Goony Bird" transport plane were closed, Jack was motioned aboard. The duty petty officer said, "This must be your lucky day. Deal didn't make it for this flight."

Jack grinned his reply, "Sure is my lucky day. I'm outta here back to the States. Deal will just have to find his own way."

An hour after takeoff, Chief Benson made a phone call to base communications and asked the duty petty officer whether any squadron messages had been dropped off for transmission that afternoon. The petty officer said "Not a one, but I will let you know if any show up."

Chief Benson set down the handset and smiled, "That fucking bastard. He is off and running. He's got enough balls he just might make it stick."

His yeoman heard the chief mutter and asked what he said. Benson replied, "No not a thing, Whitey. By the way, since we won't be sending a next of kin letter to Deal's folks until the XO gets back next week, make sure the post office guys just forward Ensign Deal's mail to his next duty station -- VF-241.I don't want his folks to get "Not at this address" letters back until they get a letter from the skipper telling them the circumstances of Deal's death. And oh yeah, let me see the copy of Dell's orders to Pensacola. I want to add a note to it before I mail it."

Tomorrow he would draft the next of kin letter and conveniently lose it in the inevitable confusion that would result between his drunk skipper and the returning XO. That night at the Chief's club, Chief Benson lifted a can of

Blatz beer and silently toasted John Deal and Jack Dell. "It is guys like you that made the Navy what it is and made it possible for guys like me to survive -- and still believe we are serving our country." Two weeks later Chief Benson collapsed at the same bar and died of a heart attack on the way to the base dispensary. His skipper had been detached five days earlier and returned to the United States for hospital treatment of an unspecified illness. The XO had many other problems to worry about when he returned and the memories of Jack Dell and John Deal vanished as if they had never existed.

Chapter 3 - Crucible

The C-47 "Goony Bird" was in and out of the equatorial showers as the pilot tried to find a hole in the cumulus clouds and let down. He was several hours out of Efate in the New Hebrides and was attempting to put his plane down on Tavabatu. It was dicey business because some of the clouds were "full of rocks," as aviators referred to the cloud enshrouded peaks of the Solomon Islands. It was up and down, diving down through the holes, only to have to circle upward again to a safe altitude in what passed for clear air. Up and down was bad enough but the turbulence of the nearby thunderstorms was enough to lift the flight crew out of their seats.

Back aft it was worse. Half of the sixteen passengers had their faces in barf bags and were spewing their guts out. The crew chief swore at his tender bellied charges as he went hand over hand to check the crates lashed down in the middle of the aisle that separated the two rows of inboard facing canvas passenger seats.

"Move your fuckin' feet, I gotta get by or you'll have a five hundred pound crate on your lap." This said while he viciously kicked aside the legs of one young sailor who looked every bit as green as the web seat he was trying to sit in.

A nearby officer passenger who was apparently dozing through this commotion with his hat over his face spoke in a clear firm voice just loud enough to be heard through all the commotion.

"You kick that swabbie one more time and I'll tear

your balls off and throw them out the hatch."

The crew chief, a burly petty officer, looked at the source of this threat and using the steel cargo strapping tool in his hand started a vicious swipe towards the officer's knees. He got no farther than four inches from his target before he found a strong hand behind his head and was swept off his feet. As he came down on the deck, his nose was shattered against the piping that formed the framework of the nearby empty passenger seat. He staggered to his feet with blood streaming down his dungaree shirt and snarled, "You son of a bitch, I'll have your ass for that, officer or not. But as he raised his hands to his nose, he felt a hand on his crotch and heard the officer's raspy voice saying,

"Careful, I've got your balls. Just a twist and they're outta here just like I said. Now are you going to quiet down and leave the passengers alone, or do you want to join the ladies choir? "The response was a groan as the crew chief fell into the nearby seat and put his head between his knees.

The officer who had initiated this mayhem, carefully undid his seat belt and bracing himself against the deck cargo, slowly worked his way forward to the door to the pilots' compartment. Opening the door, Jack Dell said with an innocent smile, "You guys having a good time? I can tell you your passengers sure as shit ain't. There is more puke and blood back there than I've seen since my last college beer bust. If you don't get this bird down soon, the trip will be wasted because these guys are ready for the hospital."

As the pilot fought with the control yoke, the co-pilot turned, and returned the smile with a toothy grin saying, "OK wise-ass, save your good news for after we put her down."

Jack Dell took this response good naturedly and answered, "Oh yeah I nearly forgot. Looks like your crew chief fell down and broke his nose. He seems to have fallen while assisting a passenger. Anything I can do to fill in for him back there?"

This question got the pilot's attention. Diving for a break in the clouds he said, "Yeah see what you can do for Pug. It's not like him to fall down on the job. We're likely to need all the help we can get -- up here and back there. Main thing I'm worried about is that fuckin' cargo breaking loose. We didn't have a lot of time to lash it down in Efate before we left."

Jack nodded and started aft. As he passed by the injured crew chief he warded off a blow to his balls and smashed his fist down on his assailant's hand to a howl of pain. "Damn, you sure are a slow learner. You just sit quietly. Since you have hurt yourself in the line of duty, I have been told by the pilot to take over your job -- so I will need that cargo strapping tool." Jack ripped it out of Pug's hand to another gasp of pain and proceeded aft to check the remainder of the cargo.

Thirty minutes later they were on final to Tavabatu airfield. Jack said with some emphasis to his passengers, "Now all you motherfuckers make sure your seat belts are fastened and stay fastened until we come to a complete stop and I tell you to get out. If you have any questions about all this, I am sure Pug here --you all right, Pug? -- will tell you it would be a good idea to do exactly what I tell you."

At that point, the Goony Bird touched down on the four thousand feet of steel Marston matting that served as the duty runway. The thundering rumble of noise of the plane's wheels as they rolled along the steel mat drowned out all further conversation. Water splashed up off the runway as high as the cabin windows and there was little to see. Welcome to Tavabatu! As the pilot cleared the runway, Jack kicked open the door to the pilot's cabin and shouted, "Pug here is going to need an ambulance.

He's hurtin' and not makin' much sense. Seems like he believes he was assaulted and he keeps threatening an officer with bodily harm. I think he'll get over it, but he does need to see a doc quick before he hurts himself some more. He sure deserves high marks for entertaining this sick group of swabbies back here while you guys tried to get us here in one piece." With that observation Jack kicked the door shut.

As the field ambulance pulled away with a raving Pug White, Jack looked up into the steady rain and struggled into his poncho. Several of the debarking passengers came up to Jack to tell him that they saw what had happened on the plane, expressed their thanks, and were prepared to say that if there was any trouble from Pug they would swear that Jack had been assaulted first.

Finally Jack had a chance to look around at his new home. It wasn't much. Lots of Marines, dogfaces, and a few sailors. Airplanes of every type, size, and description.

Many of them dead where they were parked, badly torn up or stripped of parts. The rain and mud suggested that if one stepped off the steel matting, the result would be to stand calf deep in slime and puddles. The atmosphere was foul: damp and a fetid smell that was a mixture of human excrement, rotting vegetation, and aviation gasoline. Two Army P-38s were taxiing out slowly to the end of the runway for take off. The twin in-line Allison engines made a strange purring sound compared to the rackety-rack clatter made by the Pratt and Whitney R-2800 radial engines of the Hellcats and the throaty cough of the Wright R-2600s of the Grumman Avengers.

Jack thought to himself, "This has got to be the asshole of the world. Who the fuck would fight over this piece of shit? And I have already laid myself open to trouble. Fists again, not thinking. What the hell do I care if that fat asshole picks on that kid? None of my business." But as Jack thought about it, this outburst was different. For a change he was trying to help someone, not fighting just for the joy of it. Even so, he had gotten a little pleasure in hitting that smug bastard who played god at someone else's expense. "Christ, I've got to stop this stuff. Now!"

An hour later, Jack got off the battered and muddy jeep at a set of duckboards that served as a rough sidewalk to a tent that had a crudely lettered sign above the flap stating: "Here stagger the best fuckin' fighter pilots in the world." As Jack hefted his B-4 bag and suitcase from the back of the jeep, he smiled. "Just what I like: a modest group of shipmates who have kept their sense of humor."

In the doorway he found himself being looked over by an officer in a skivvy shirt and a pair of khaki shorts. He had no socks on, just an unlaced pair of boondockers. He held a damp sheaf of papers in his hands. "Well come in, don't they teach you to come in out of the rain in flight training? You must be a fuckin' replacement. What kept you?"

Not waiting for an answer this semi-dressed gentleman turned around and walked into the tent. Jack followed and watched his host seat himself in a chair with a sign behind it that stated: "Skipper, VF-241." Under the sign, there was an additional shingle that stated "Lieutenant Gus Prather." But between the first two words a piece of paper had been inserted with the single word "Commander."

So this was Lieutenant Commander Gus Prather. As Jack took in the scene and presented John Deal's packet of orders, flight log book, and service record, he looked over the man behind the desk. Sandy red hair, bloodshot eyes, hollow cheeks, an unhealthy pallor -- malaria? too much quinine? -- a days growth of beard, grimy hands. But eyes that burned right through you, looking for weakness, searching for evidence of junior officer smart ass, asking "Do you measure up?" Obviously Prather had been an athlete at one time, but the slack muscles were atrophying into fat in the gut, the jowls, and the upper arms. Nevertheless, he still transmitted a sense of power and he clearly was not a guy one messed with.

Jack believing he had to say something, said, "Ensign John Deal, reporting as ordered, sir. And sir, I'm called 'Jack.'"

Prather did not reply and just left Jack standing while he tore open the packet of orders and John Deal's service record. He quickly flipped through the pages and then looked at Deal's flight log book. After five minutes of this, Jack started to shift uneasily on his feet while a small group of officers congregated on the other side of the tent. They were making themselves busy, but they just as clearly were interested in what the skipper was going to say to the new guy.

Finally Prather looked up with a frown on his face and said. "Well Mr. Deal -- you have to earn the name 'Jack' since you and I ain't on a first name basis -- ain't much here for me to feel good about. An only child -- but you don't get on with your parents. Didn't do well in College. Joined up with the rest of the pack after Pearl Harbor. Apparently, you fucked your way through flight training, just doing enough to get by. I get the idea that you want to fly your way -- not the Navy way. Maybe got a wild hair that will get yourself killed some day. The Japs may save you the trouble. What is there in here that tells me you're a lady's man? Won't get much fucking out here -- unless you find a tender sailor that you fancy. If you do, you won't get off this island alive, I guarantee it. Anything, I've missed, Mr. Deal?"

Jack fumed silently under this assault, his face grew crimson, and he tensed his muscles resisting the urge to sass back -- and confirm that he was indeed a smart ass with more lip than sense. The injustice of it was a blow. He hadn't counted on having to answer for Deal's many shortcomings. His own were bad enough. There was a temptation -- resisted only with great difficulty -- to give a macho answer: "Just put me in a plane, sir, and I will show you what I can do." He knew Prather would knock that sally into left field: "Your record doesn't tell me you come completely equipped with a lip also!"

Through his rage he marveled that Prather had come up with a pretty good thumbnail sketch of John Deal -- all without knowing he had pranged himself at Kahoolawe in a stupid assed accident and without having read the letters in his seabag as Jack had. Pretty good at sizing people up. Will not be able to fool this guy for long. Best to go along for now and see what happens.

Jack groped for an answer to all this and satisfied himself with,

"Sir, I haven't seen a piece of Navy paper yet that told the whole story -- and told it straight. I only ask that you look behind the paper and make up your own mind."

"Bravo, Sir Galahad! But I have made up my own mind and the count is one strike and no balls -- well maybe two balls. We'll see if you can get on base in this ball game. Nobody believes Navy paper and never fear we'll see soon enough who the real John Deal is -- and whether he is smart ass lip or a pilot who can work with this outfit and stay alive. The XO's over there -- he's the ugly bastard who's scratching his crotch -- he'll get you settled in. I want to see you tomorrow morning after we get the first launch in the air. That's all for now, Deal."

The next two days Jack spent talking to individual pilots in the squadron. The talk was tactics, how the squadron's new Hellcats differed from those back in Lahaina, the way to get out of and back into Tavabatu without getting your ass shot off by trigger happy anti-aircraft crews, and the hygiene of survival in the tropics. Jack was assigned to a tent in "Boy's Town" with five other ensigns and "JGs." He found that his bunk had belonged to an ensign who had been killed ten days earlier. Went in inverted after a fight with a couple of Zekes who had his number. Welcome to Tavabatu and naval aviation.

Jack found that only with a great deal of effort was he able to head off the smart answer or the flip comment in the days that followed. He worked hard to avoid giving his squadron mates any leverage over him beyond the one of experience that they already enjoyed. His answers to questions were direct and honest. He didn't volunteer any information and discouraged inquiries into his personal life. He bided his time until he could get into an airplane.

His squadron mates quickly typed him as a loner and after a number of aborted attempts to get him to open up, gradually left him alone. Jack had time to explore his new surroundings. VF-241 was the only Navy squadron at Tavabatu. It was there only temporarily while transitioning to Hellcats from the old Wildcats and waiting for a base to become available further up the Solomons chain. The field was run by the Army Air Corps. Some New Zealanders and Marines were also present. The VF-241 area was comprised of a collection of twenty tents and one Quonset Hut (for radio and weapons maintenance) and a flight line dispersal area for the squadron's 25 new Hellcats (of which only 16 were serviceable). A makeshift "officer's club" was under one of the tents. The bar was a set of old packing cases backed up by a wheezing ice machine and cases of Australian beer.

The rain that greeted Jack on arrival at Tavabatu continued. When it lifted for a brief interval, the hot, humid, and sour air was enough to make him gag. Mud was everywhere. Life was a constant battle to escape it: the route to the heads was surveyed to keep mud on boondockers to a minimum. It was an unpardonable sin to track mud onto the floor boards of the tent (shoes were left at the entrance and thonged shower shoes or "klaks" were put on). Ground crews lifted pilots from the jeep up to the cockpit to avoid tracking mud into the plane (inverted flight could provide a shower of dried mud and blind a pilot at a critical moment in combat), and the worst thing that could happen was for mud to appear in one's chow or bunk.

The food was the usual forward area Navy stuff: reconstituted milk (when it could be obtained), canned meat ("spam" or "Vienna sausage") and vegetables, rice or potatoes, canned fruit and the occasional pie made from it, and kool-ade, lemonade or tea. Soggy crackers, over-age chocolate bars that came out of the package with a white sheen on them, and "fresh vegetables and greens" that quickly went limp or turned yellow with mildew completed the menu. The mildew was everywhere: on shoes or anything leather, on clothes hung or packed too closely together, and in any enclosed area out of what sunlight there was. Life was a curious blend of fastidiousness to frustrate the adverse effects of the environment and crudity to concentrate on the essential and jettison everything else. One's best uniform (rarely worn) was a set of wash khakis with the insignia of rank on them. Combination ("bridge") caps and dressier uniforms soon rotted away and were consigned to the base dump. It was a world of basics (clean socks), small and rare luxuries (mail and a shared bottle of scotch), and some moments of great excitement (a Jap raid, mail call).

Jack was left to cool his heels for four days before he found his way on to the flight schedule -- and that just for a short familiarization flight around the field. He knew in his heart that Prather was testing him. Trying to see if his patience was up to watching everyone else fly twice (or more) a day, seeing if he would have too much at the bar (Jack had one beer and soon left for his bunk to read dog-eared pulp fiction), and observing how well he took advice and instruction. The inactivity was starting to lick him when Prather called him to his tent.

"Sit down, Deal. I've got to find a place for you in this outfit. You start your real flying tomorrow morning. You'll be flying wing on me. That's no honor and it ain't easy. I'm putting you there because I want to look you over and see if you can do what you're told. We'll be up for morning CAP. There is nothing fancy in doing combat air patrol around here. You just stay on my wing as close as a flea -- but not too close. Your job is to not just look -- but to see. Keep Jap assholes off my six. No heroics and stay off the goddam radio unless you see Japs or I'm about to be blasted by one of them. One final bit of advice: when you stop learning in this business, you start dying. Don't take anything for granted and don't think you have all the answers. The guy who lives longest around here is both lucky and a good student. I don't think you are either. It is up to you to prove me wrong."

Jack's reply was simple, but without any emotion. "Yes sir. Is there anything else?"

Prather's reply was as close as he ever got to amiability: "Get your ass out of here and see you on the flight line in the morning."

It was pitch black when the flight line jeep came to pick him up at 0430. The sailor in the jeep handed him a fried egg (reconstituted!) and rancid bacon sandwich and pointed to a thermos of black coffee as he spun the wheels in the mud and bumped and splashed along to the flight line. He was met by the plane captain, a kid seemingly young enough to be a baby brother. "Good morning, Mr. Deal. Good to have you aboard to spit some death and destruction at these godless Japs! Let me help you with your gear. The plane is pre-flighted -- I have been around her twice. No need to get your butt in the mud -- sir."

The sailor's cheerful greeting was in such contrast to the surroundings that Jack asked him his name. "Whitey Hansen, sir. And sir, I was on the plane you came here on -- coming back for what passes for R&R at Espiritu Santo. It was a neat thing you did to the big fuckin' crew chief. You already got a good rep with the white hats in the squadron. And thanks."

Before Jack could respond, Whitey thrust a Navy "yellow sheet" -- a brief summary of the his airplane's recent repair and flight history -- in front of him and asked him to sign it as he held a red lensed flashlight on it. "You must have done something to charm the skipper to have him schedule your first CAP flight at 'o-dark-thirty' and then fly wing on him. You got your work cut out for you -- sir."

Jack grunted and mounted the step up to the Hellcat's wing and sat himself in the cockpit. Whitey helped him strap in while Jack used his flashlight to check around the cockpit. In ten minutes he had started the engine and began to taxi out following Gus Prather who exited the adjacent revetment and headed for the end of the takeoff runway. Two more Hellcats fell in behind Jack as each "S" turned down the taxiway to keep the plane ahead of them in sight over their F-6's long noses. The only lights shown were the planes' blue formation lights and the red and green wing lights. None of these lights were directly visible from behind. Each pilot had to rely on the loom they reflected in the humid air to keep from overrunning the plane ahead. Jack could sense the prop of the plane behind him getting ready to chew into his tail feathers. It was an eerie business.

In daylight they would have made a formation takeoff in pairs on the narrow matting that constituted the runway, but with the first twilight on the eastern horizon, they had been briefed to takeoff singly at five second intervals. Jack watched Prather pour the coal to his plane and start rolling. A full throated roar and long blue exhaust flashes marked Prather's Hellcat as it gathered speed and vanished down the runway. Five seconds later Jack turned

onto the runway, locked his tailwheel, and put h
up to full power. The thrust pushed him back into
and he had to force himself to push forward to
lock of his shoulder straps and see over the nose. U
rudder gingerly he somehow kept the plane on the
runway and lowered its nose as his airspeed built u
plane lifted off smoothly and he throttled back
starting to look for Prather so he could join up. He
what had to be him off the port bow as Prather mad
one hundred and eighty degree climbing port rendez
turn. Soon his formation lights came into view and
saw the outline of Prather's Hellcat against the eastern s.

Jack completed the rendezvous by pulling
smartly on the inside of Prather's turn -- some thirty f
aft and ten feet stepped down -- and then slid smooth
under Prather to take up his "free cruise" position on h
starboard side. Within seconds the other two aircraft in the
division joined up but remained on Prather's port side. It
was almost as though they were attached to Prather's
Hellcat by a rubber band: no tricks, just crisp disciplined
flying.

Daylight came quickly and Jack suddenly realized
that he hadn't closed his canopy after takeoff. Without
taking his eyes off Prather, he sheepishly grabbed it with
his right hand across his chest and slammed it closed with
his left elbow. "Stupid-assed mistake! Congratulated
myself on a simple rendezvous and stopped thinking.
Won't do. Think ahead, dammit!" His mind was taken off
his embarrassment by Prather's firing a short test burst
from his guns. Jack was supposed to test his a split second

later following the skipper's example, but had forgotten to throw his master armament switch and charge his guns. After a short delay he fired his test burst, followed almost at the same time by the number three and four aircraft. Another embarrassment. Two mistakes already.

Trying to think ahead he loosened up his tight formation on Prather and concentrated on looking for Japs. All he saw was one hell of a lot of planes taking off from Tavabatu and a flight of Army B-17s passing high overhead probably headed for Rabaul. Listening to the radio he heard Prather check in with the "AIRSOLS" fighter director at Henderson Field on nearby Guadalcanal. No substantial enemy activity -- but a report of a Jap float plane snooper in the area an hour before.

About an hour into the flight -- the sun was now up -- the fighter director radioed "You will have company. Many. High. Bearing shackle WVA unshackle. Distance shackle LN unshackle. Help on the way."

Prather immediately started a climb on the bearing given by the fighter director. A few minutes later Jack could see many Hellcats -- and some Army P-38s far below climbing out of Tavabatu on the same heading. The enemy was now 75 miles away and closing fast. It would be up to Prather's CAP to get an altitude advantage and attack the incoming raid while the CAP just launching got into the air and gained sufficient altitude. It would be an uneven scrap for a while at least.

In five minutes Prather lowered the nose of his aircraft and eased his throttle back to fast cruise setting as his division flew in a loose formation with four sets of

eyeballs scanning the horizon. At 28,000 feet it seemed very quiet as the humming of the four engines receded from the pilots' thoughts and they looked around the as yet uncluttered horizon. Jack thought, "Just a day's walk in the park!" After a few minutes of this solitude Prather pointed down and ahead to his left and Jack saw at least two vees of 5 Jap Bettys each moving along like sharks at about 20,000 feet. All closed up and teeth bared. The only question was where were the inevitable escorting Zekes? No time to find out. They would show their hand when Prather engaged.

Prather was already turning left down sun and diving on the Bettys in a high side run. Jack opened out to the right to enable him to keep an eye on Prather while still scanning for any accompanying Jap fighters. The second pair of Hellcats moved out to the left and lined up on the most distant vee. As Prather pushed over Jack saw the first of the Zekes attempting to break up the attack. They were slightly lower and were arcing around to intercept. Jack keyed his mike: "Lion leader, Lion two, bandits, three o'clock low. About six of them. Over."

Prather responded: " I gottem, but they're too late for this run. After I finish this pass, you break right and I'll split S out of here. Come around and cover my six. Got it?"

Jack rogered the order and saw Prather start shooting. Christ he was climbing up that guy's ass. Pieces started to fly off the Betty and its port wing dipped. As Jack broke right per his orders and Prather went inverted and started his dive, Jack saw the Betty blow up. But he had little time to look at the fire ball because he was sucking the stick back in his lap in a six "g" turn and looking for the Zekes. Sure enough, a pair was diving after Prather. Jack rolled out smoothly around on the tail of tail end charlie of the pair and fired a short burst. Too far away for good shooting, dammit! The Zeke started to turn away and Jack followed in on the unalerted Zeke leader.

"Lion leader, Lion two, bandit closing on your tail. I'm at his six. Pull up and I can splash him."

There was no answer but Prather pulled up and the Zeke followed him. As Jack predicted the distance between his Hellcat and the Zeke closed rapidly. Jack's prolonged burst tore the Zeke apart, with one wing falling off and the plane twisting like a pinwheel as it started down. "Holy shit!" Jack had little time to reflect on his kill because someone was on his tail and his bullets were smacking into his fuselage like sledgehammers. And then they stopped.

"Lion two this is Lion leader, you got your head up and locked. There were two planes in that pair. The one you spooked by firing too quick just about had your ass. You owe me one."

By this time the sky was full of aircraft: Zekes, Hellcats, Lightnings, Bettys, and a couple of stray Kiwi Kittihawks. No sooner would Prather line up on a Zeke and Jack would have to warn him off because another was on his tail. And so it went for fifteen more minutes as the sky was crisscrossed with contrails and black smoke from falling aircraft. Then just as suddenly as it had started it was over. No Jap planes to be seen. Lion aircraft quickly formed up on Prather. Jack was late joining up and had to settle for the four slot in Prather's division. Prather noted that none of the Lion aircraft keyed their mikes, although there was a lot of talk among other aircraft on the same frequency.

Returning to Tavabatu via the prescribed route the flights entered the "break" point in right echelon by divisions over the duty runway at 250 knots. Prather broke smartly starting his sharp turn and slowing before his landing gear started coming down. Others broke just as smartly with drill-like precision. When Jack's turn came he did the same but somehow ended up wider abeam than his three predecessor aircraft, and he had to crab back in to get a little above and behind number three. The landing was uneventful, less than five seconds between each aircraft -- except for Jack with his ten second interval.

After taxiing into his revetment, Jack shut his engine down and started to look at his aircraft. It was a wreck. Large holes in the after part of the fuselage -- fortunately not near the control cables and many bullet holes in the wings. Whitely Hansen climbed up on the wing and asked him how it all went (this with a big grin).

"Looks like Grumman Iron Works saved my ass. I really got worked over -- but you shoulda seen the other guy!"

Prather was already in his jeep waiting." As soon as you finish that chat, Deal, we got to have a conversation. Get your ass down here."

Fifteen minutes later, after a piss and a glass of cool tea, Jack could feel himself calming down from his "combat high." His muscles gradually relaxed and his knees stopped shaking. The returning pilots had gathered in the briefing tent. The tent flaps were all up to let in what breeze there was. There were four rows each with five collapsible chairs lined up facing a crude lectern with a blackboard behind it. It was obvious that no one ever took the trouble to erase the blackboard and just wrote over whatever was already there. Groups of pilots were talking and with a liberal use of hands were describing their fight. The air intelligence officer in the corner of the tent was debriefing each pilot one by one.

When Prather walked in, the conversation ebbed and gradually died away. He turned and stared at his pilots as they scrambled to take their seats. He seemed to make eye contact with everyone in the tent. There was no emotion showing on his face. His first words were.

"Not bad (long pause in which smiles broke out)......But not good either (eyes cast down on the deck). It took too long for the squadron scramble to get off and join the fight. You all couldn't have been in the goddam head jettisoning that neat breakfast this morning (this to the tune of the rumbling of at least half a dozen stomachs)."

A loud belch was heard from the last row of chairs. Prather immediately fixed the culprit with his piercing eyes and snarled, "OK you shithead, now that you have farted through your mouth, let's hear you whistle through your asshole. Anybody else that has any funny stuff to add can be debriefed by me personally later."

This sally brought some shuffling of feet and then

dead silence. "As I was saying: too long to get airborne. XO you've got to carry the can for that. When you are on the ground, I don't ever want any of you more than five minutes from the cockpit. If the maintenance crews can have the birds ready -- and they always have -- you can always be ready to fly them unless you are on the binnacle list."

"If you have to straggle into the fight, join up in twos and fours first -- even before you start climbing. Single birds at the right altitude are worse than sections and divisions at the wrong altitude. Obviously, I demand that you be joined up and at the right altitude. But sometimes you have to choose. A single bird is like trying to screw with a limp dick: there is a lot of action but no satisfaction." As Jack listened to Prather's tirade and his last metaphor, he wondered if this is how the famous "Pratherisms" were born. Prather had the ability to make the point in easily understandable -- and memorable -- terms. Prather went on to critique the squadron's gunnery: "Shooting too far out. You got to get in so close you can see that Jap gunner's eyes. If he doesn't fill your windscreen, you are too far away. You don't screw while sitting across the room from your lady, and you don't screw Japs that way either."

Prather let this sink in and then added, looking directly at Jack as he spoke, "When you shoot early you give the guy a chance to break and get on your ass."

After fifteen more minutes of this, Prather toted up the score. "Looks like three Zekes and three Bettys. Should have been twice that. I started my run on the

Bettys too late trying to get up sun. The result was I got into a little tail chase and only had a crack at one Betty. I should have got two. Before you break from here and get debriefed by your division leaders, I want each of you bastards to think hard and long and list in your own mind what you did wrong today. That's all. I'll debrief my division in my office."

Prather's office as we have seen was nothing more than a corner of the squadron office tent. Packing boxes had been located in such a way as to give him a modicum of privacy. But Prather's voice was loud enough to carry to the adjacent tent to say nothing of beyond this makeshift partition.

Prather's debrief of his division was every bit as meticulous as his debrief of the squadron. He started by making sure he had everyone's attention. "Why is it that I have to be the eyes of this outfit? Why couldn't someone else have spotted those Bettys 20 seconds before I did? Even when Deal here called out the Zekes, I had already had them for 10 seconds. You should be looking at the sky not my wingtip! If you can't look and fly wing on me at the same time, open out until you can see. We are only going to live if we have four sets of eyeballs looking for those bastards."

Turning to Bertie Reynolds the leader of his second section, Prather said, "Bertie, you broke too wide when we went down on those Bettys. I admit I didn't set you up too good for that run, but you got to compensate for the skipper's mistakes. You ended making a tail chase even longer than it shoulda been. Good shooting on that first

Betty. But in all honesty we each should have had two of those fuckers. Now get out of here and tell Cy what he did wrong and how you are both are going to get it right next time."

As Bertie Reynolds and Cy Denton left the skipper's "office," Prather turned to look at Jack. Jack returned Prather's stare without emotion -- he didn't lounge but he was not sitting erect either. His demeanor bespoke curiosity rather than fear or arrogance. Jack was determined he was going to keep himself under control. But he was also sure he wan't going to let Prather intimidate him. It was a difficult line to walk and he hoped he had it right. "Pretty proud of yourself? Flaming a Zeke on your first CAP mission? And that was pretty cute telling me to pull up, knowing the Zeke on my tail would have to pull up too to give you an easy shot. Not very often I get manipulated by my pilots to provide them a better shot while I am getting my ass shot off. Maybe it was an easy shot -- but it was good headwork using my ass as bait. I will do the same for you someday.

"But it is hard for me to believe that the John Deal that got such lousy gunnery grades in training could make that shot on his first flight. You are either good, lucky, or a fast learner. We'll soon find out which it is. You still got to convince me that the John Deal recorded on Navy paper is the same John Deal who got a Zeke today.

"Now let me tell you what you did wrong -- it may take the rest of the morning but I will try to keep it short. First, you were late joining up. I expect my wingman to join up early in my rendezvous turn, not when I roll out of it. And that was a stupid assed mistake leaving your canopy open after takeoff. It cost you 15 knots and 5 gallons of gas and you may need both next time. Didn't the guys tell you how we test our guns around here? As soon as you join up on my wing your master arm is on and your guns are to be ready for test firing. And we do that starting in sequence with me and then you and so on to number three and four. The evolution should be so fast that number four has started before I stop. This is a test of smartness and tells me how alert my division is.

"I already told you to look for Japs not my wingtip. You know where I'll be, but you don't know where the Japs will be. The guy who fills in the gaps in his knowledge the quickest lives the longest. It is that simple.

"No complaints with how you followed me down on the run on the Bettys. But as you know the Zekes were right behind us. Your job in breaking after the firing run is to get on the guy who is on my tail while I go after the guy who is trying to get on your tail. You stood around too long congratulating yourself on flaming that Zeke. Meanwhile the guy you spooked by firing too soon is getting on your tail. Fortunately for you I looped around and got him before he completely wiped you and your bird out.

"The rest of the fight was just a game of grab-ass. You weren't much worse than the rest of these ballet dancers. Too much flying and not enough shooting. We'll get better soon or we'll all be dead.

"And, oh yeah, you broke too wide coming back into the field. We don't have that five second landing interval just because it looks good. Someone else may need to use the duty runway -- in a hurry. It's your job to get down quickly -- and quickly to me is a five second interval. And don't go smart ass and give me a three second interval either. I don't want your prop chewing up my ass just because you got to show the skipper what a fucking hot shot you are. OK, get outta here and let me get back to work. And, oh yeah you'll be launching again this afternoon so don't unpucker your asshole yet!"

As Jack left the skipper's office he marveled at how Prather had handled the debrief. He started with the squadron, then to the division level where each division leader debriefed his own team, and finally to the section where each lead pilot debriefed his own wingman. The content of each debrief was specific and oriented to correcting mistakes. Nothing was overlooked. He worked hard to destroy complacency and sloppiness. No mistake went unremarked. He accepted blame himself and fearlessly laid it on others when warranted -- even embarrassing his XO in public if he goofed in the air. There was no personal animosity. He got their attention and then laid it out for them. Moreover, each pilot left the debrief with an aphorism or metaphor that he would remember and repeat in the future. A colorful but masterful performance by a craftsman.

The only sour taste Jack had was that he was having to carry the can for that fuckup John Deal. He wondered if he would ever live down that bastard's reputation. But when he thought more about it, he ruefully acknowledged it was the price he had to pay for taking over another guy's life. "Who told you it would be easy? You were happy to execute John Deal's orders. Don't bitch now that you have to live his life. A pound of flesh for a pound of flesh." But Jack didn't know then that there was more to taking over John Deal's life than living with his lackluster training command record. But he was soon to learn.

When Jack had been aboard for two weeks and a month after leaving Lahaina he received two letters. One from the queer in San Francisco and one from John Deal's girlfriend, "Maggie Fitz." The letter from the San Francisco cocksucker he burned. He didn't want it read by anybody. The letter from Maggie rocked him back on his muddy boondocker heels.

It started out gently chiding "Dear John" (how ironic!) for not writing. But she quickly went on to telling him how much she loved him. She said that she had missed a period and from the way she felt she just knew she was pregnant. She was both happy and worried. Happy to have something of John to remind her of their love for each other, and worried that her parents would soon find out. To hold off that day she had changed jobs and rented an apartment in Bakersfield -- all over her parents futile objections. In her gentle way she asked what John wanted to do about all this. Did he want her to abort or to keep the child? Did he still have the same feelings for her that she had for him? Did they have a future together?

Although Jack had experienced a hard-boiled upbringing and been a party to many one night stands, there was something about the letter that nagged him. When he analyzed his reaction, he realized his response was on two levels. First, it would not do for Maggie Fitz to contact the Navy or John Deal's relatives (if she knew who and where they were) and start a big scene that would jeopardize his already tenuous hold on John Deal's persona. But on a second level the letter touched him in ways he never thought possible. Here he was in a spot where each flight could be his last. There she was not knowing the father of her child was already dead. And not knowing what a complete SOB John Deal was.

At the first level he needed to sweet talk Maggie Fitz along so that she wouldn't make waves that would carry him home to face the music orchestrated by a defrauded Navy. At the second level, he thought: What the hell, why not tell the girl I will marry her? She had enclosed a portrait photo of herself and she was indeed a knockout -- with a type of beauty not fully captured by the snapshots in John Deal's seabag. He saw the choices and flipped a coin: heads for a hard line and tails for a soft line. Tails it was and he started to ponder how he could write a meaningful letter to a girl he had never seen, never written to, and propose marriage in a letter written in his own (not John Deal's) handwriting.

Inspiration solved the problem. He pecked out a letter on one of the squadron's old creaky typewriters. He made the excuse that he had slightly injured his writing hand and had to peck out the letter on a typewriter. He examined John Deal's signature in his service record and scratched out a creditable "Love, Your John" at the end of it. In the letter he acknowledged his (John Deal's) paternity, his hope that she would keep the child to term, and marry him as soon as he returned to the States. Jack sealed the letter, wrote the privileged "Free" on the envelope where the stamp would normally go, and personally delivered it to the squadron intelligence officer who performed most of the mail censorship duties. In turning it over to the intel officer, Alf Sundstrom, Jack told him that the letter was very personal and pleaded that not a whisper of it be divulged to anyone. It was a common message for Alf who merely replied in his stoic Minnesotan way, "Don't worry, I'm already carrying around so many fuckin' secrets that one more will simply go into the shit bucket."

A week after posting the letter, Jack got his second kill. It was almost too easy. It was a snooping Emily flying boat limping home with an engine shut down. As luck would have it, Prather had a problem charging his guns and elected to coach Jack down to get the kill. The tail gunner was already slumped over his gun and all Jack had to do was line up dead astern and pump a five second burst into the cripple. It was more than enough and the big seaplane pitched up, then dived nearly vertically, and finally disintegrated into a fireball. There was no pleasure in it.

The ease of the kill was not enough to head off a scathing critique at the debrief by Prather who prodded Jack as to how he would have handled the Emily if the tail gunner had been alive. And not liking the answer had proceeded to wirebrush a subdued John Deal. But as the weeks went by, Prather's criticisms began to subside and lose some of their sting. Jack had helped Prather through a very rugged fight with a swarm of Zekes and Vals, assisted Prather in getting two kills, and managed one for himself. Jack's self-enforced (with great difficulty) quiet and unassuming demeanor had started to garner some respect from his squadron mates. Where before he had been an unknown quantity, he was now seen as a steady wingman, and a killer in a down and dirty fight. The day word of his promotion to Lieutenant Junior Grade came through, he notched his fourth kill. There were pilots in the squadron with twice his time at Tavabatu with no kills, just pleased to be alive and have a "probable" to their credit.

He was forced by custom to "wet down" his new silver bars -- though few pilots wore any rank insignia at all -- by buying the drinks at the bar that night. As Jack Dell he would have gloried in the affair, but as John Deal, now "Jack" Deal, he found it all forced and of little interest. Prather showed up and after a brief bit of jocularity at the bar retired to a table to talk to the XO and Alf Sundstrom. There was a new pilot who had just reported in that day. Peter Schaffer, a short wiry "JG", had come through VF-321 at Lahaina some six weeks after Jack had left. Schaffer looked steadily at Jack through the evening and took advantage of an opportunity of catching Jack alone to strike up a conversation. "Glad to meet you. Apparently you are off to a great start in this outfit. Got lots of good words from these guys to just do it like Jack Deal does it and everything will be O.K. I hope you will give me some advice on how to break in here."

Jack just nodded and said, "Just listen hard and don't say anything and you'll be OK. I've been lucky."

But Schaffer had something else on his mind. "Christ, 321 was the most fucked up outfit I have ever heard of. Target fixation was always being talked about. Got the guys so jumpy they would pull out of a dive before they really got started. Seems like a bunch of folks had creamed themselves over two or three months at Kahoolawe. One of the guys had a name that sounded like your -- John Deal or Dells or something like that. Ever run into him?"

Jack was ready for it and answered as nonchalantly as he could, "Yeah Dell was there but not for long. He and I were always getting taken for the other. Nobody stayed there long in those days. Are Skipper Womble and Chief Benson still there?"

Schaffer thought for a moment and then said, "I think Womble left a month before I got there. If Benson was the admin CPO, he must be the one who died of a heart attack about the same time. Shit that outfit had more casualties in their offices than on the flight line."

Having diverted Schaffer from his original curiosity, Jack heaved a sigh of relief that the two people who could have really blown the whistle on him and his new identity had left his life -- probably forever. Jack had no intention in getting into a drunken conversation with Schaffer and have the subject come up again so he steered the newcomer to a group giving a rousing rendition of a sea-chantey with obscene lyrics. Jack knew that he was living on borrowed time and that sometime soon he would be in grave danger of being exposed. In the meantime he intended to stay alive and beat the odds.

Several days later Jack got a letter from Maggie and some dunning notices for unpaid bills back in the States. He took Maggie's letter back to his bunk and toyed with it wondering whether to open it before or after his next flight. He elected the latter. He almost tossed out the dunning letters, but then thought better of it and put them with Maggie's letter to be read that evening.

The mission of the flight was to fly cover for about a dozen "turkeys" going up to hit the Jap airfields at Buin. It was no milk run and was Jack's first escort mission. Prather briefed them carefully, where to position themselves relative to the lumbering Grumman TBFs, what to do if they were jumped, probable Japanese tactics for diverting the escort while they cut up the bombers, and so on. The whole affair ended up confusing Jack. Instead of being aggressive, they were to be defensive. Don't go after the Japs, they're probably decoys. Keep plenty of altitude. Always hold something back for the next fight. A perfect mission was one where not a bomber was lost. If you shot down Japs but lost a bomber you had lost.

Twelve Hellcats and eight New Zealand P-40s were on the launch. The P-40s low with the bombers and the Hellcats high. The turkeys lumbered off first, their awkward landing gear folding outboard into the wing instead of rotating aft as in the F-6s .They soon joined up and began their turns towards the northwest. The fighters followed. The P-40s because of their short legs could only go about two thirds of the trip. For this mission the

Hellcats each had a 150 gallon drop tank to give them enough for some fighting fuel over the target. Another group of Hellcats was to meet them on the way home to pick up the escort job.

The flight started simply enough: one turkey and one Hellcat abort, but the Hellcat abort was Prather and the XO took over. This led to a shuffle in the batting order. Otherwise a smooth ascent to 20,000 feet for the Turkeys and P-40s and 25,000 feet for the 11 F-6s .Jack was the number four in the XO's division. In some ways it was a relief not to have Prather along. The XO had a reputation for being easy going, although Jack had learned to his cost when he had doped off on a simple ground job that the XO's sting could be very painful. Still in the air and flying number four on a JG who was little more experienced than he was gave Jack the feeling he could relax and enjoy matters a bit-- XO's division or not.

As they neared the target area the turkeys, now escorted only by Hellcats, started their power glide down to start their bombing runs. Almost on signal, the Zekes appeared high on the northwest horizon barreling down from Rabaul. There must have been twenty of them. It turned out that Jack must have seen them first, because his "tally ho" caused the XO to turn roughly to an intercept heading to place his planes between the Japs and the turkeys and to order the jettisoning of the flight's drop tanks. The plan was to have the first two divisions led by the XO conduct the intercept and the remaining division, now down to three aircraft, look for the inevitable second bunch of Zekes.

As the first two divisions approached the oncoming Zekes at about the same altitude the XO ordered Lion flight to fan out to execute a division size scissors -- force the Japs to make some choices and hopefully some mistakes. They chose to do neither and headed directly for the turkeys thus giving the Hellcats the choice of a fleeting head-on shot or a flat deflection shot. The port division of F-6s tried the head-on shot and then pulled around sharply to get on the passing Japs' tails while the starboard division started their turn early to come around and make a flat approach on the now descending Zekes. The result was that the air to the northwest of the turkeys' target was full of aircraft violently maneuvering to avoid collision or from getting "sucked" into a tail chase.

It was a case where both opponents had been surprised by the other's actions. The XO had thought the Zeke leader would peal off several divisions to deal with his and let the others bore into the turkeys. The Zeke leader thought he could accept a head-on attack by the F-6s and then leave them "sucked" while he wrecked mayhem on the bombers with his entire force. He hadn't counted on being screwed early and late by the scissoring Hellcats. He paid a stiff price -- five Zekes going down in flames before the turkeys had been engaged. But the rest swarmed in, fortunately in some cases with a Hellcat on their tail.

The rest of the fight was a wild mêlée. Jack found he and his wingman caught in a scissors by four Zekes. They tried all their tricks but would no sooner get free and start to get on the tail of one of their tormentors when another pair of Zekes would start to work them over. This went on for several minutes until the remaining three hellcats on high escort entered the fight, bagged one of the Japs, and ran the rest off. They then closed up on the turkeys who were diving with several Zekes weaving in among them. They arrived just in time as the Avenger formation was starting to fray. The attacking Zekes turned their attention to the Hellcats but didn't have their hearts in the fight and soon left. Just as Jack was about to line one up in his sights on a straggler among the departing Japs he swore he heard Prather whisper over his shoulder: "Sucker! What the fuck is your mission? Get your ass back to those turkeys."

Jack turned back in complete frustration. He had hardly fired a round in the fight. He had been all over the sky -- most of the time trying to save his own ass. And here he was supposed to be an intrepid escort! He gradually calmed down as the surviving turkeys and F-6s counted noses. They had been bloodied. Two turkeys and one hellcat missing. Another Hellcat was smoking and kept dropping out of formation. The pilot was barely hanging on. He finally had to head down looking for a place to ditch. There was nothing they could do. They had just enough fuel to get back to Tavabatu -- and still had turkeys to escort.

It was a glum group that gathered in the debriefing room. Prather sat in the back row and let the XO go through his debrief. It was clear that no one had a clear picture of what had happened. The only good news was that a "Dumbo" Catalina flying boat had picked up one of the pilots who had been shot down. As the debrief wound down, Prather got to his feet and after his usual stare and pause said, "You got your asses kicked. You can't do it all over again, but you can sure learn from it. After you finish your division and section debriefs, I want to talk to each of you -- one on one. That's all for now."

Jack's turn came that afternoon. Prather asked him simply, "What happened, Jack?" It was the first time Prather had addressed him that way and Jack relaxed feeling his skipper wanted him to talk man-to-man. "Skipper, I know we play the hand we are dealt, but for starters there simply weren't enough of us to cover all the bases. Once we saw the Japs we closed them aggressively -- now that I think about it, too aggressively. We played their game -- we were going to get one pass -- and that a lousy head on. After that we were sucked in a tail chase all the way and they were all over us. It became a matter of saving our own asses rather than taking care of the bombers."

Prather nodded and asked what would you have done? How like Prather: learn from it, don't bitch about what can't be changed. Jack knew he was being tested.

"Sir, I wouldn't have closed the Japs -- I know I am second guessing the XO but shit that is how it is -- I would have used that minute or two to get a little more altitude and then I would have followed them down as they pushed over against the bombers. With the extra altitude and our speed advantage we would have caught them before they got to the turkeys. Because they were bunched I would have had every guy take one Jap -- I know that means breaking wingman discipline. Besides the Japs were bunched up enough that we could easily join up after that firing pass because we would be coming off first.

"After that first pass I would have told everyone to pull up and join up over the turkeys and wait for the rest of the bastards to show up. If the high CAP hadn't already started in, I would have them follow any Jap stragglers in. I would have....."

Prather held up his hand, "That's enough. You did everything right except splitting up the sections with every man for himself. Rather than do that call down the high CAP to follow you in. They weren't doing any good up there and you were already outnumbered about two to one."

"Jack, we lost a damn good guy this morning. Bertie Reynolds has been with me from the beginning. I should have sent him back to the States a month ago. He deserved it. He won't be going back now. You're taking his place as leader of the second section in my division. The only critique I have of your performance today is that I suspect that you were sitting back fat, dumb, and happy as number four waiting for things to happen. I wasn't there so I can't say why you didn't get a good shot in that fight. You shoot well enough and you keep your cool -- most of the time. In spite of the hard time I've been giving you, I think you may be a fighter -- even a killer -- and lord knows we need all we can get.

"OK get out of here, I got to talk to the XO and try to pull all the stories I've heard today into something that hangs together."

Jack left in a daze. Prather had talked to him man to man. Missing the fight today and then learning that it had been botched clearly had taken its toll. Jack had never seen him so depressed -- almost licked if he didn't know better. Maybe Prather should be the one going back stateside.

As Jack threw himself on his bunk, he remembered the letter from Maggie and fumbled for it until he found it.

Dear John,

You have made me the happiest girl in the world! That you want our child too and that you still love me just started me to balling. I am so happy! It is like a great cloud has lifted from my life and I have a reason to live -- and to look ahead eagerly to when you can come back and we can start the rest of our lives together. I love you and our baby so much I could just shout it out to the world. Please put up with my gushing, but I have to share my happiness with someone!

There was more -- much more -- but Jack put the letter down." Holy Moses! I've done it now." But he felt a secret pleasure that he could make the lovely girl in the photograph happy. He wondered what it would be like to hold her in his arms at a moment like this. That shithead Deal would never know, and wouldn't know how to handle it even if he were still alive. Jack knew that he would have to write a response -- and he dreaded it even though there was some bittersweet pleasure in it. He wondered when all was done how he could face this girl -- even by mail and tell her that he was Jack Dell not John Deal and that John Deal and the father of her child was dead. Maybe he wouldn't live that long -- or something would happen so that he wouldn't have to face that prospect.

In the months that followed his correspondence with Maggie increased in frequency and Jack began to look forward to the distinctive blue envelopes (with the light scent) that came in the mail every week or two. He received a package of cookies and personal items from her -- the first time he had received a gift from anyone. The occasion was John Deal's birthday and he had forgotten all about it. As the correspondence continued he started to sense a change in his attitude. She loved him -- or the person she thought of as John Deal. He heard about the changes in her body with the pregnancy -- first heartbeat, a swelling abdomen, tender breasts, telling her parents, and on and on. The intimacy was one between husband and wife. He found that he cared for this sweet girl he was deceiving (the only consolation was that he hadn't done her as much damage as John Deal had).

He was not too surprised when in one of Maggie's letters she raised the possibility of a marriage by mail. One of her friends had done it -- to a boy in the Army serving in Italy. Would he consider it if she were to send the necessary forms to him? She didn't want to push him but she felt they owed it to their child. As Jack thought about it, he gradually came to the belief that it would do no more harm than had already been done. So he wrote back agreeing and asked her to send the forms.

While these letters crossed the Pacific Jack was into his sixth month in the South Pacific and had notched his seventh kill. He could tell he was a different man:

steadier, less impulsive, more calculating, taking more care with his words before he spoke, unwilling to respond to an insult (whether intended or not). And he began to feel some empathy for the married men in the squadron. He would offer compliments on the photos of a wife and child and feel a secret wish that he could share his thoughts about Maggie with a squadron mate.

He had received a spot promotion to full lieutenant -- engineered by Prather. The latter had made Jack a division leader as he had become a true old hand in the squadron. He had moved up the seniority and theater experience ladder as attrition and transfers back to the States took their toll on the squadron roster. But he found himself getting restless. The quality of the Japanese opposition had declined noticeably. It seemed that some of his opponents were more interested in aerobatics than actually fighting -- a fatal mistake before Jack's guns.

In time he received the marriage forms from Maggie. They had to be notarized. He had no choice but to seek a private meeting with Prather. He told Prather that his girl was pregnant and that he wanted to marry her. Prather looked up from his desk and fixed Jack with a stare.

"Jack, I'm delighted that you are doing what people call the 'right thing.' But somehow I don't believe you're giving me the full story. Someday if we both live through this mess, you need to buy me a beer and tell me everything. Sometimes I think I know who John Deal is and sometimes I don't. But anyway, congratulations. I wish we could spare you to go back and do the deed in person.

I must say I admire your ability to carry this personal problem over the past few months and not let it get in the way of your flying. Here, I've notarized this marriage application for you and I look forward to getting the news that you have a son or daughter. On second thought, leave it with me and I will put the censor stamp on it and get it in the mail so these snoops don't learn what they don't have to know."

Three weeks later Jack received a letter from Maggie saying they were married and that she was due any day. Seeing no point in keeping it all a secret any longer and wanting to get the evidence of his marriage in his service jacket in case he was killed, he stood the drinks at the bar that evening. In a strange way it made him more of a part of the fierce sense of brotherhood that was animating the squadron.

The next letter from Maggie was given to him after he had marked up his tenth kill. Two divisions led by Jack and Prather had creamed a formation of Japanese bombers that had done everything wrong. Maggie announced the birth of their son, John Fitzgibbons Deal, while the squadron was in the process of moving its base of operations up to Munda. Two weeks later Jack was scheduled to fly his last flight with Prather before the latter was ordered back to the States. The mission of last flight was to escort a large group of Army B-25s on a raid on Buin.

There was little air opposition, and that easily dealt with. Some of the new guys in the squadron had a chance to get their first kills. Jack and Prather had their two divisions on high CAP and were not needed. As they zoomed down to rejoin the departing bombers some flak started to open up and exploded with uncanny accuracy among the closing fighters. Jack heard a sound like a sledgehammer hitting the side of the plane and then felt a searing flash of pain in his right calf. The pain was so excruciating that he bent double against his unlocked shoulder harness. Looking down he saw a spurt of blood from his leg. When he tried to raise it off the rudder pedals to look at it he saw that it was broken and that he appeared to have a compound fracture.

He reported to Prather that he had been hit but that airplane seemed to be flying OK. He had to stop the blood spurting or he would never make it back to base -- still over an hour away. Groaning he released his knee pad, removed its securing bungee, and strapped it around his leg just below the knee. Then he took the handle of his survival knife and used it to twist the bungee taut until the blood flow subsided. Several times during this process, he nearly fainted.

Prather saw him slumped over and told him to open his canopy to get some air in the cockpit. With a great effort with one hand and elbow he managed to do it and it cleared up the fog before his eyes. The rest of the way home Prather talked him along -- keeping him conscious and doing his thinking for him. On the landing Jack ground looped off the runway because his leg was powerless to use the needed right rudder.

An hour later in sickbay he was visited by Prather. "You got a nasty chop to that leg and the only question now is whether you get air-evacked to Australia or the States. I've told them that it has to be the States. Your tour is almost up anyway."

Jack started to protest, and then realized that he owed this man too much to brush away a final favor. He fell back into the bed and held out his hand and croaked. "Thanks skipper. Thanks for everything -- giving me a chance, riding me hard because I needed it, and for being a big brother" Jack felt the tears come to his eyes and turned away. He hadn't cried since he had been ten years old. Prather, touched his shoulder as he started to leave. "Don't forget, you owe me a drink when all this is over."

He never saw Gus Prather again. Prather was killed in a kamikaze attack while he was serving as the executive officer of a carrier off Okinawa in the spring of 1945.

Chapter 4 - Homecoming

The trip back to the States was mercifully short as Jack began to appreciate the way the Navy pulled out all the stops for men wounded in combat. He was whisked from Tavabatu to Efate to Fiji to Hawaii to Hamilton Field north of San Francisco. Five days after leaving the Solomons he found himself in Oak Knoll Naval Hospital near Oakland, California, and in the hands of surgeons who pondered what to do about his leg.

As short as the trip was Jack had plenty of time to think about his future as he flew home. Fortunately, he had prevailed on Prather, and the XO who had relieved him, to delay for several weeks sending the wounded in action message to Maggie, who was now his "next of kin." He told them he would see her soon after his arrival in the States.

Between bouts of unconscious sleep as the painkillers took their toll he reviewed his situation. He had taken John Deal's place in the Navy while keeping Jack Dell "alive."

Jack Dell's pay had been sent to his checking account in Eugene. He had drawn an occasional check on the account over the past six months. During an R&R trip to Efate Jack had visited the local paymaster and had (as Jack Dell) drawn his back pay and shifted his allotment to Maggie. The disbursing clerk had hardly noticed the discrepancy between his marriage certificate name and his pay record name.

Looking back to his weeks in Hawaii, there seemed

nothing to worry about there. Putty Benson was dead and Jake Womble was being dried out somewhere. No death messages for John Deal had been sent to the Bureau of Naval Personnel or next of kin. So far as the large naval bureaucracy was concerned both Jack Dell and John Deal were still alive. He didn't know if Naval Air Station, Pensacola, would ever find out that an Ensign Jack Dell was on his way to them. But he also suspected they wouldn't care. Personnel clerks never had to go looking for problems; they came unbidden.

There had been a nagging worry about his health record. A curious hospital corpsman would notice that the description of John Deal did not match the description of the man on the examining table. Too many discrepancies. Jack solved that problem by having an accommodating flight nurse in Efate mail some "personal effects" home to Eugene. The loss of his health record was only discovered while he was on the flight to Hawaii. He was not the first combat casualty to arrive at a naval hospital without his health record.

The real threat to his continuing deception was running into someone who knew either the real John Deal or the real Jack Dell, and having that someone take enough interest to blow the whistle. He would just have to take his chances with that. Of more concern was his personal situation -- particularly the one that would develop when VF-241's wounded in action telegram reached Maggie in Bakersfield. He knew that his time was measured in days. Inevitably, she would come to visit him in the hospital. He knew that he had to control the conditions of the unavoidable confrontation and he couldn't do that while a patient in a hospital. The only way to make it all work would be to get leave to get down to Bakersfield before the medics started carving on him to give him back the full use of his leg.

But, how to orchestrate this reckoning? He must face Maggie and tell her the whole story. He knew that in so doing he was putting his life in her hands: exposure to a Navy who would court martial him on a variety of charges including defrauding the government, false official statements, "conduct unbecoming" and so on. He also faced a civil action by Maggie for fraud for impersonating John Deal and doubtless other "high crimes and misdemeanors."

So he must face a Maggie who did not yet know that he -- her correspondent in the Solomons -- was in fact Jack Dell, that John Deal had been killed six months ago, and that she was married to a man she didn't know. It was important that the meeting be conducted one-on-one, so that he could persuade her that her (and his) best course of action was to leave matters as they were and continue the deception to the end of the war when he would be mustered out and hopefully put it all behind him.

What would Maggie do when confronted with the facts? Although her letters had started to give him a measure of the wife he hadn't met, he knew that the warmth generated in the letters could not survive the shock -- and anger -- about how she had been treated first by John Deal and then by Jack Dell. Jack came to realize that the deception of his double identity to this point had been the easy part. He could concentrate on his flying and put the deception in a quiet corner of his mind -- responding to a weekly letter from Maggie while fearing exposure by some old Navy acquaintance. The former had become pleasant and the latter was unavoidable. Now he was faced with a real woman with a real son, who looked forward to a reunion with a real husband.

Jack wondered if he had anything going for him. He was convinced that he was a better man -- whatever that meant -- than John Deal had been. His mind went back to the many letters to John Deal that he had read -- letters from sluts and a queer. He had married a pregnant girl who if the truth had been known would otherwise have been a single mother, a terrible burden even in wartime. He had a good combat record but he dismissed it as irrelevant in something as personal as marriage. He had come to care for the girl he wrote to and hoped some of that caring came through. Would she accept him as her husband long enough to get a divorce? Would she go right to the cops? Only one way to find out: go down to Bakersfield and face the music.

But first he had to get by the Navy Medical Corps whose motto seemed to be that once they had your body, they wouldn't let go of it. The initial diagnosis was that he would need more surgery to make up for bone and flesh loss in his right leg. But they agreed -- reluctantly -- with him that surgery could wait until he had a week with his wife. So, on a December morning in 1943 he caught a Greyhound bus to Bakersfield. It was a painful ride with little room to stow crutches and a leg in a cast below his right knee.

Jack was in uniform -- a new one and not very well fitted since almost everything he owned had been left behind in the South Pacific. He wore his combat ribbons, a Distinguished Flying Cross with two additional stars, an Air Medal with several stars, a purple heart, and the usual service ribbons that went with service in the Pacific. He won the approving looks of his fellow passengers and the bus driver who wondered about the gaunt, intense, and apparently preoccupied "war hero" on crutches who rode south with them through the San Joaquin Valley.

On arrival at the Bakersfield bus terminal he got a taxi, stopped at a liquor store to buy a fifth of the best wartime liquor he could purchase, and went on to Maggie's apartment building. Since it was a Saturday he thought the odds would be good that he would find her home. Navigating with great difficulty he gradually made his way up the stairs to her third floor apartment. Standing in front of her door he could feel the sweat break out as he attempted to control his labored breathing and collect his thoughts. He knew that the next few minutes were critical to his future. Pausing a few moments, he rang the doorbell. He faintly heard a baby crying as footsteps approached the door.

As the door opened he saw a lovely blond girl of slightly over average height. Although slender, she was clearly still in the process of shedding the few extra pounds acquired during pregnancy. She held a whimpering infant in one arm and was buttoning her blouse with her free hand. The look on her face was a charming combination of annoyance and expectancy. She waited for Jack to speak.

"Are you Maggie Deal? I'm from your husband's squadron. I would like very much to talk with you."

She looked into his eyes, and then to his crutches, and finally to his legs. Her voice caught as she said, "Has something happened to John? "Is he all right?"

Jack's nod to this last question seemed to reassure her and she said, "Please come in. I'm sorry to keep you waiting in the hallway. I'm in the middle of nursing little Johnnie here and I have forgotten my manners." She stood back from the door and let him enter. He noticed that he was in a small apartment that some would call "modest" and others would call shabby. But its most distinguishing feature was the obvious fact that this was an apartment furnished to support an infant. There was a small crib, a bassinet, a baby carriage, piles of diapers, a box of toys the boy wouldn't be ready for until he was a great deal older, and the usual paraphernalia associated with caring for a new baby. The odor of fresh milk, talcum powder, and diapers left no doubt as to focus of the occupant. The healthy and hungry baby Maggie was carrying was not only emotionally the center of her life, but it provided the physical -- even sensual -- focus as well.

"I'm sorry about the appearance of this place. I work during the week and Saturdays and Sundays are my catch-up days. Would you excuse me for five minutes while I finish nursing him and put him down for a nap?" Not waiting for an answer she went through a door that led to the bedroom.

Jack took the opportunity to look around the

apartment. He put the package of liquor in the small kitchenette and returned to the front room. There was a little desk in the corner and he noticed several of his letters on it. There was also a small snapshot of John Deal that Jack had taken from Deal's seabag and sent on to her. It was abundantly clear that Jack would not pass for John Deal.

Jack found a chair and gently eased himself down in it to await Maggie's return. After a few minutes and several weak cries from Johnnie, she reentered the room. She had found time to comb her hair and put on some lipstick. She was brimming over with questions. Jack held up his hand to stop the torrent in mid-sentence.

"Maggie, I have a long story to tell you and I will need your help to get through it. It is not easy for me to be here, but when I am done you will see -- if not fully understand -- what has happened and my part in it."

Her response was some alarm on her face, alarm that gradually softened to a look of concern when Jack smiled briefly.

"Your husband and I went through VF-321 in Maui together. I did not know him at all since we overlapped only about a week and it was a big squadron. People were constantly reporting in and being detached. He must have met you just before he went to Hawaii."

She nodded and tears came to her eyes as she twisted a small handkerchief in her hands.

"Maggie, John Deal was killed in an aircraft accident seven months ago, the day before he was scheduled to leave for the South Pacific."

Unable to restrain herself any longer, Maggie went to the desk and held up the sheaf of letters that Jack had written to her. "You are obviously wrong because I heard from John just last week! We were married two months ago. I just started getting a government allotment as his wife. Surely the Navy isn't paying dead men." She smiled at Jack through tears as though he were badly addled and needed sympathy instead of anger.

"Maggie, please hear me out. This is a complicated story. I know John is dead because I packed up his personal effects for shipment. I have the letters that you and others sent him before he was killed. It is hard for you to hear that news from a complete stranger and it will take time for you to accept it. I wish I could make it easier, but the easiest way is to tell the truth as best I can."

"Well, what about these letters, including one I got from John last week?" she said with some spirit -- as if she held the trump cards.

"Maggie, I wrote those letters because I took John's place on the day he was killed. Although I gather John didn't write to you much -- maybe not at all -- after he left you to go to Hawaii last spring..." Jack looked at her as though it were a question and then continued, ..."He probably wrote to you in longhand. You will notice that all the letters since have been typed. You didn't receive notice of John's death because as far as the Navy was concerned at that time, you were not a next of kin."

Maggie stole a look at Jack's hands looking for some sign of injury. She looked up with a stubborn look on her face, "Well, if I'm not married to John, who am I married to?"

"You are married to John Deal, more exactly, the man who is masquerading as John Deal. I am Jack Dell. It is a complicated story but I took John's place the day he was killed. I had been ordered home to the States -- in some disgrace I might add -- and wanted a chance to redeem myself by getting into combat and doing well. By a series of coincidences and some deception on my part I managed to take John's place and was sent to the South Pacific where I started to respond to letters that the real John Deal could -- maybe would -- never answer."

At this Maggie put her face in her hands and burst into uncontrollable sobs. "I simply don't believe it. Someone should have -- would have -- caught you and somehow I would have been informed. What kind of monster are you? Taking the place of a fine man, the father of our son, a man ready to go to war. A caring, sweet, gentle man who I loved. You son of a bitch, I ought to call the police now and have them take you away!"

As Maggie said these words Jack saw that there was a great deal of toughness beneath the feminine wrapper and that she could be a very determined woman and deadly adversary. He wondered whether John Deal had ever known that woman existed. She clearly was fighting for her life -- a life that Jack Dell had entered without measuring the full consequences of his actions.

Jack said, "I'm deeply sorry. I had no role in John's death. I took his place -- for my own selfish reasons -- and went out to the war. Your letters, particularly the one telling John you were pregnant, got to me and I convinced myself that there would be no harm done in continuing the deception. Later as our letters continued I found myself caring for the brave girl who was unmarried and faced with a pregnancy. I tried to give you some hope by first asking you not to abort the child, and then later agreeing that we -- that is John and you -- should get married. That way the child would have an acknowledged father and you would have some support if I were killed as John was. What started out as a selfish deception on my part grew into something more solid. I began to look forward to your letters as a connection with a life and love, something new to me."

"But you knew that someday I would find out. That the whole house of cards would come falling down and that I would end up worse than I started!"

"I came here today for two reasons. The first is dishonorable. After I was wounded, I knew that I would be sent back to the States. There was no way to continue our correspondence. The second reason is that I have learned a lot from my commanding officer, who has been like an older brother to me. And I learned a lot about courage and love from you. I have come to realize that I have to confront you and tell the truth -- and accept whatever decision you make when you know the facts. Until I got to my squadron I had very little to be proud of in my life. I have been a brawling, unruly, and selfish kid with a chip on his shoulder. You can expose me if you will -- and I will admit to every point -- even though you should know up front that my deception will be difficult to disprove on the basis of Navy records."

"What are you suggesting, Jack Dell? That we should now become man and wife and Mr. and Mrs. Jack Dell? That you are the father of my son sleeping in the next room? That we should go through life living a lie -- so you can build up your combat record and escape paying for a misspent youth? That we should pick up as though nothing has happened this afternoon except that a strange man has turned up at my door who says he is my husband? Had you planned to sleep with me tonight? Do you really think I am a loose woman because John Deal didn't take decent precautions on the one night that I slept with him? In spite of my letters to you, you really don't know me at all! But I think I know you. You are a schemer, an ego-maniac who thinks the world exists for his convenience and pleasure, a man who now thinks because he says 'I'm sorry' he should be forgiven and provided a fresh start in life -- a life of lies."

Jack took this onslaught with a bowed head and to say the least, a heavy and contrite heart.

"Maggie, I agree that I am all the things you say I am. I don't offer any excuses. All I ask is that you not decide quickly. That you weigh the consequences of your decision carefully. In the eyes of the law and the Navy you are Mrs. John Deal. Your son is John Fitzgibbons Deal. The government has a contractual obligation to you both to take care of you in the event your husband is killed. It is true that it didn't cost me anything to take on the obligations of a husband, but it will if we leave things as they are. Since you find me so repulsive -- and I understand how you feel -- you can initiate divorce proceedings and avoid living the lie that you describe. At least Johnny will have had a father and a name, a name that I will do my best to see he will be proud of...."

"Spare me the lawyerly rational Jack Dell. I'm fully aware of the trouble I'm in. I hardly knew John Deal, but I suspect now that he was an SOB. I started to feel good about myself again when he-- you -- started to answer my letters. I felt, I was loved by a good man, a man who was probably better than the one I remembered, a man who had matured as he got into the war and became responsible for someone besides himself. All of this has crumbled in the last hour. Now I probably have neighbors who in all likelihood observed you come through the door (whispers, "Her husband is home!") and are waiting for the bedsprings to start to squeak. You are right, I need to think. I need to get out of here and think."

Almost on signal a whimper came from the next room as Johnny Deal started to wake up. Startled, Maggie left her chair and went to get her son.

Jack called, "I brought some scotch. Is it OK if we have a drink to let the dust settle a bit?"

"Go ahead, I can't while I'm nursing. The glasses are over the sink." As both returned to the room, Maggie with an obviously hungry Johnny in her arms and Jack with three fingers of Black and White in a glass, they looked at one another. Maggie with a look of mental exhaustion and vulnerability -- her eyes red from weeping, Jack with a look of embarrassment and contrition. Almost simultaneously, they said together, "What a damn mess!" And then each looked away.

Jack said, "Why don't we go out to dinner? We'll take Johnny after you feed him and give us both a change."

She sighed, "Why not. I don't have any suitable food in this apartment anyway." The upshot was that a half an hour later they were on their way to the best restaurant in Bakersfield in Maggie's tired pre-war Ford sedan.

The dinner was a mixture of success and failure. Maggie would burst into tears as she thought of her past and future and then seem to come to terms with the reality of Jack Dell as John Deal. She plied Jack with questions. What did he really know of John Deal? Was he an OK guy or a make-out artist who was also a lousy pilot? Jack squirmed under such questions because it would be a cheap shot to tell Maggie about the real John Deal (even though he had his letters and records to back him up). On the other hand what did he owe the SOB who had screwed up Maggie's life? He managed to have it both ways, saying something good about John Deal while leaving enough blanks to where Maggie being the smart girl she was could easily draw her own conclusions.

Finally he told Maggie bluntly, "There is no percentage in tarring the reputation of your son's father even though he was no angel. I have my own opinion of John Deal. I've been living his life for six months, and it hasn't been easy. For the first three months in my squadron I had to fend off brickbats intended for John. Let's just let the real John Deal rest in peace. We need to worry about Maggie Deal and her son."

As Jack ordered coffee, Maggie asked, "You could have just not answered my letters, couldn't you? It would have just been a case of one one-night stand among many. It wouldn't be the first time a girl had gotten knocked up and the guy just closed down the letters. I wish I knew how much your decision to answer was based on self-interest and how much on caring for a girl in distress."

Jack had no answer for her and none was needed because Johnny woke up at this point. Jack paid the bill quickly and they went back to Maggie's apartment. By the time they arrived Johnny was squalling demanding dinner. At the door, Maggie said, "You might as well come in, all the neighbors have heard this ruckus."

This time she didn't use the privacy of the bedroom for nursing, she just sat down in the rocker undid her dress, released her nursing bra and put a very large breast where Johnny Deal could quickly use it as nature intended. "No point in squeamish modesty. I am a married -- if somewhat fallen -- woman. It's not the first teat that you have seen."

For a while she rocked Johnny as Jack looked on with some but diminishing embarrassment. Gradually, Johnny's dining subsided and Maggie hoisted him for a few burps and then took him into the bedroom and put him in his crib.

As she came out the door, she looked at Jack and said, "I've reached my decision. You have yourself a wife and son, like it or not. And it won't be easy. A couple of things you need to know up front: No bedroom privileges for you, not now and probably not ever. Second, I may still decide to divorce you. And third, I may still decide to expose you. But for now I am going to go along with you

Lieutenant Dell. You can make a bunk on the sofa for tonight. You may hear me bring Johnny out to the rocker during the night so that I can feed him. You signed up to be a father and now you get to pay the price."

Jack smiled back at her said, "I guess John got the honeymoon and I got the rest of it. I'm ready to take my medicine, Mrs. Deal. I've got to go back to Oak Knoll tomorrow afternoon. I'm going to have some surgery on Monday morning to see if those sawbones can straighten out my gimpy leg. Good night."

Lying back on the sofa with the lights out, Jack thought that the day could have been worse. Maggie Deal was a handful in more ways than one. A sixth sense told him that she was something more than "a girl in distress." He sensed that she had "been around." He wondered what the full story was on Maggie Fitzgibbons. Anyway, a marriage to her would not be easy, but it might be exciting. He considered what she might be thinking as she lay in her bed with her son next to her in his crib and her "husband" banished to the living room sofa as though they had had a fight. He wondered if time would heal as he wandered off to sleep with his leg throbbing.

Chapter 5 - Recovery

Jack went into surgery Tuesday morning instead of Monday morning. He was barely conscious as the nurse wheeled his gurney back to the surgical ward. She smiled at him. "Well Lieutenant, one more hurdle. Looks like you are going to be as good as new thanks to the miracles of medical science. Some of these guys that we got from civilian life are master craftsman with a scalpel. You're lucky. In the meantime, you are off your feet until I say you can get up."

Jack's recovery was swift, helped a great deal by a better diet than he had at anytime over the past year -- and much less alcohol per day. Two weeks after the operation he was told that he had visitors and was wheeled out to the visitors' lounge. There he was met by Maggie who wheeled in Johnny in a small baby carriage. She came over and pecked Jack on the brow, whispering, "That's for appearances -- so people won't talk." She gave him a forced smile and then sat down beside him.

Jack responded with a trace of a smile, "Good to see you, courtesies or not. I'm the only guy who hasn't had any visitors -- till now. Any second thoughts about our bargain?"

She shook her head and then looked down. "I guess I didn't realize how far out on a limb I had put myself. I'm sorry that I let loose at you the way I did. I can see a little more clearly now that you did more than you had to, self interest or not. I think I have to say my jury is still out on Jack Dell, but he's still in the dock. I also need to tell you that the five hundred dollars you left to take care of expenses was badly needed. I think I am self sufficient, but I am still thinking like a girl who only has to look after herself. I --- we --- have a son to look after."

Jack put out his hand for her. She looked at it just for a moment and then tentatively put her hand in his. He said, "Thanks friend. I think you are what I have needed. Too much time here for me to think, think about what an asshole I've been. Thanks for understanding and giving me time to get myself straightened out."

As Johnny chose this moment to come awake, Maggie reached down to pick him up. When she had him in her arms, Jack asked, "Can I hold him? I need to get the feel of him. My arms are OK, it is my legs that are the problem."

After a moment's hesitation, she handed him over, fussing about his blankets and cautioning Jack not to handle him like a football. More fussing occurred and then they both sat silently while they held hands and Johnny cooed and gurgled. Neither felt the need to talk further. The talking had been done for the day. This continued until Johnny got restive and wanted dinner. Doing his best to provide Maggie some privacy in the busy visitor's lounge, Jack watched his wife and her son coo to one another.

As Maggie made ready to go for the long bus ride back down to Bakersfield, Jack said, "I think they will give me four or five days convalescent leave next weekend. I would like to spend it with you. Am I welcome?"

She shook her head. "Jack, I have to think. I have a job, a baby, and a banged up husband I don't even know. I haven't got it sorted out yet. "Give me some time -- please."

Jack persisted, "If you don't want me in Bakersfield, will you and Johnny come up to San Francisco? I think special services here can get us some rooms at the Mark. It would give you a chance to get away."

She responded by leaning over and kissing his cheek. "I will call you by mid-week and let you know. Good-bye." As she turned to leave, she added, "Where do they get these nurses? They are knockouts. Don't forget you are a married man! " The last with a half smile as she disappeared out the door pushing Johnny in the carriage.

She called on Wednesday night and said she needed more time. The weekend was out. Jack went into deep depression and only started to pull out by Saturday as he viewed the prospect of spending the Christmas holiday weekend in Oak Knoll. One of the younger nurses had taken a liking to him and he could tell that he was close to falling off the edge. At eleven o'clock Saturday morning he was told he had visitors. But instead of being taken into the visitor's lounge he was wheeled down a long passageway to an office marked "Commanding Officer." He then was rolled into the waiting room outside the Hospital Commanding Officer's office. While he wondered if this meant he had been exposed as an impostor, he got out of his wheelchair and using his crutches was shown into the office where an elderly captain greeted him. "Glad to have you aboard Lieutenant Deal. We have a couple of surprises for you. First, if you turn around you will see your wife and son coming through the door.

He saw Maggie, looking radiant, her long blond hair swinging gracefully and walking with her model's walk that combined grace and sensuousness. A Navy nurse pushed Johnny's carriage. Maggie came over and gave him a kiss on the lips that was as sweet as it was unexpected. It was moist and soft and full of promise. He was stunned and only dimly in the background heard the CO continue his welcome.

"......And second we have an award for you." He held up the blue box. Jack thought how like the Navy to screw up a personal moment with some mickey mouse ceremony....

He then heard a voice that droned, "the President of the United States takes great pleasure in presenting the Navy Cross to Lieutenant John Emerson Deal, United States Naval Reserve, for heroism as set forth in the following citation........"

Jack was stunned for the second time in thirty seconds. That SOB Prather had worked to get him a Navy Cross that truth be told Prather deserved if anyone did. The award was for the flight in which Jack had shot down two zeros and gotten two probables while "at great risk to himself had come to the aid of squadron-mates under determined attack by the enemy...."Horse hockey! He had only done what Prather had taught him to do. This train of thought was interrupted by a flash bulb as the ever present Navy photographer was there to immortalize the occasion.

Jack thanked the CO, and asked that there be no publicity because he "wanted to surprise his parents even if he couldn't surprise his wife and son. Please no publicity at all." The last with such emphasis that the CO nodded to the photographer who shrugged as he left. The assembled group clucked that this just showed how modest this hero was. Maggie who knew the score had her habitual half smile on and chimed in, "Yes, please let us make it a surprise!"

The CO turned to his desk, and said, "One more thing, Lieutenant, I have got the surgeons to agree to give you a five day shore leave and our special services department has somehow found a way to get you a five day stay starting tonight through Christmas at the Mark Hopkins for you and your family. We all hope you enjoy it!"

With that they were ushered out of the office to applause. Jack shifted into uniform and a Navy sedan delivered them to the Mark for the long weekend. As they checked in the desk clerk, obviously very old and recalled for the duration, said,

"We are honored to have you as our guest Lieutenant Deal. We are very proud of you and your family. I trust you will find everything in your suite to your liking. The champagne is with the compliments of the management. Oh yes, because we are sure that you and Mrs. Deal would like to see the town, we have arranged for an experienced person to stay with your child. Just call the concierge when the need arises. The bellman will see you to your suite. Good day sir and I hope you enjoy your stay with us."

The suite seemed like heaven to them: an expansive

view of the bay, luxury all around them -- unlike a tent at Tavabatu or a cheap apartment in Bakersfield. After the bellman had stopped fussing with the luggage and refused a tip, they were left alone. They stood alone in the center of the room, the view ignored for the moment. Jack reached out and took Maggie's hand and then reached for the other as he leaned on his crutches.

"Well, Mrs. Deal. Is this an end or a beginning?"

"Damned if I know Jack. Why don't we break a rule and see if there are bubbles in that bottle of champagne. I don't think Johnny will mind this once. His father doesn't get a Navy Cross every day."

The rest of the day was a joy. After feeding Johnny, they left him in the hands of a sitter with a bottle, and walked out of the suite hand in hand to a day of shopping and sightseeing in San Francisco. Making allowances for the fact that it was wartime the city was at its festive best for the Christmas season. Both tried to put the past behind them and live for the present. They found themselves laughing together at nothing that would have been funny to someone who had observed the scene. But at one serious moment, Maggie turned to Jack and said: "You know that this is not real, Jack. We will have to pay the price someday for today's fun. But we have got to have some fun while we can, before the real world closes over us. I just wanted to tell you that as giddy as I am, I am dead serious about where we are and where we are going. But, I must say that for the first time I am glad you are here. With that she reached up, put her arms around his head and gave him a long kiss that said: "I surrender -- at least for now."

They returned to the Mark and after a scotch and water for Jack and a glass of 7-up for Maggie at the "Top of the Mark" they went down to the suite and ordered dinner from room service. Jack managed to finish the rest of the now flat champagne. As they sat at the little table in the sitting room of the suite, both became somewhat somber. Maggie looked up and said,

"I hate to see it end. It has been so much fun."

"End, hell. We have four more days..."

"Yes Jack, but the first day is the treasure."

"Is there a first night at the end of the first day, Maggie?"

She didn't answer. Instead she looked up, looked into his eyes, and held out her hand. "What do you think, sailor? No, don't answer that! I sound like a loose woman, a woman who would have a one night stand with John Deal. God, how I would like to take that night back. But if I did, I wouldn't have my Johnny -- and I wouldn't have had Jack Dell come into my life (this with a smile)."

"I have to give Johnny a late supper and then let us see how well we can behave!"

Later with Johnny fast asleep he came to her. He didn't say anything; there was nothing to say. She responded to his hand with a gentle sigh and murmured "It has been so damn long....."

It was a night of lovemaking neither would ever forget. At first there was no hesitation, no holding back, just a headlong rush to seize each other and enjoy and prolong the moment. It became clear to both within moments that neither was new to lovemaking. They knew instinctively what each wanted and joyfully gave it. When the moment came to catch their breath and enjoy the afterglow, each started the dance of mating again -- slowly and tenderly, generating a response in the other, a response that kept building until both shuddered a release that left Maggie sobbing and Jack breathless and shaking.

For a long time they held each other tightly, squeezing each other from time to time to offer their love and to reassure themselves that the moment was real. Gradually the passion subsided and Maggie lifted herself on her elbows and looked down on Jack.

"Well, now you know my secret, Jack Dell. I have been in bed before. John Deal was just one of a half dozen or so. I am not just a poor girl in distress. I am a woman who got careless and slept around once too often. And from what I can see you've been around a bit yourself."

"Maggie, I'm not keeping score. I just know I have my hands full and I love every minute of it."

"Jack, you've got to be serious for a moment. I have a confession to make. I heard you out when you made your confession in Bakersfield that Saturday morning early this month. Now, you have to hear mine!"

"OK, go ahead but I think our talents lie elsewhere."

"Jack, you remember when I sent you that letter telling you -- Johnny Deal -- that I was pregnant? I was scared as hell. I wrote that same letter to two other guys who could have been little Johnny's father. Hell, I didn't know which one of the three did the deed. But you were the only one who answered my letter. That bastard John Deal probably wouldn't have answered. So you see, I misled you and you misled me. We're even. I'm sorry as hell I put you through the wringer down in Bakersfield. I was angry and embarrassed. I had gotten what I deserved and I didn't like it."

"I'll be damned, you little minx!" He smacked her rump and then started laughing. After a moment Maggie joined in and both laughed hard enough to where they woke Johnny up. Maggie wearily climbed out of bed, buck naked, and picked up Johnny and with great tenderness put her breast to his mouth.

"Johnny, you little bastard. I don't know who your daddy is, but I love you. And I think I have found the man who will give you a brother or sister."

Jack leaned back against his pillow and enjoyed watching mother and son. He savored the challenge of loving this complex and lusty woman. A woman who enjoyed her lovemaking and loved the result as well.

After a half hour of feeding Johnny and getting him back to sleep, Maggie rejoined Jack in bed and they started again and continued until they fell into a deep slumber.

The next four days were spent half in the hotel making love -- with the "Do not disturb" sign up -- and half out doing the town while a sitter stayed with Johnny. They both glowed with the pleasure of each other's company. They ended up exhausted. On the last day, they both surrendered, Maggie saying "I am sore as hell down there and you don't look in such good shape either. I just had to be sure that I didn't leave anything for that pretty nurse back at the hospital -- the one that I think has her eyes on you!"

As Jack put Maggie and Johnny on the Bakersfield bus for the long trip home, she said, "We really need to get down to see my parents in LA as soon as you are up for travel. They didn't know John and thank god they never saw his picture. But they need to see their grandson and son-in-law."

Jack nodded his agreement and watched the bus as in drove out of sight. It was three weeks before he saw them again. By this time he had discarded his crutches and relied on a cane. The doctors said that in another two months he might be returned to limited duty and could start flying in three months if the flight surgeons gave him a check up. Although good news, Jack chafed at the delay.

The visit with Maggie's parents went better than either had any right to expect. As grandparents their eyes were on Johnny, and Jack was treated affectionately but really little more than a necessary accessory for producing a grandson. He bore up well. His only regret for the weekend was Maggie's unwillingness to make love under her parents roof. That had to wait for the little apartment in Bakersfield -- and as it turned out was interrupted by Johnny's colic. He learned soon and well the lesson of a married man: Mom likes to play with Dad, but the atmosphere is important. The presence of a relative or a sick child puts a damper on affairs! He took it all with good grace and got a certain amount of satisfaction from the fact that Johnny liked to be held by his "father." Even better, he found that he enjoyed holding him and talking to him. Maggie viewed the proceedings with undisguised pleasure.

In early 1944 Jack was released from Oak Knoll and assigned limited duty with a fighter squadron in San Diego. He persuaded (it didn't take much) Maggie to give up her job and follow him there to live in a small apartment he had somehow found in crowded wartime Coronado. Maggie's parents arranged her move. This began three months of pleasant duty. Even though Jack wasn't flying he was assigned to a fighter squadron just forming up to embark as part of USS President's air group. Jack in spite of his efforts to stay in the background (he refused to wear his ribbons) was given the special consideration accorded an ace with ten kills and a Navy Cross. His leg had healed enough by late March that he was cleared to fly again -- to his great joy -- and Maggie's alarm. By the time USS President sailed in late April Jack was in full flight status, having acquired the necessary requalification flight hours and carrier landings.

Maggie saw him off with tears in her eyes. Johnny had been coached to wave and they both saw the big ship shape a southwesterly course off Point Loma as her escorting destroyers formed up around her. Jack was going off to war for a second time, this time aboard a carrier instead of in a fever-ridden swamp.

Chapter 6 - Veteran

Jack was in an anomalous position as a lieutenant in VF-277. As junior a lieutenant as he was, he was nevertheless the second senior officer in the squadron and should have been made the executive officer -- or "XO," the number two man in the squadron. Jack wanted to avoid that job at all costs. Not interested in a career in the Navy he didn't want the visibility in the air group or the ship that being the squadron XO would involve. It was only with great difficulty that he was able to convince his skipper to leave him in the ranks of pilots with no really significant ground duties. He promised the skipper that he would loyally support whoever was appointed as XO and that he would use his time to help the "nuggets," the new pilots fresh from the training command, pick up the necessary combat skills.

The officer designated as the XO deeply coveted the job anyway. Jethro "Jeb" Stuart was an ambitious man who had developed superior skills in navigating through the Navy bureaucracy and exploiting his knowledge for personal gain. He saw himself as every bit as good an aviator and officer as the skipper -- or the air group commander for that matter. He had already planned to stay in the Navy after the war. Although not an Academy graduate he believed his true worth was such that he could not fail to be recognized in the peacetime Navy. The late assignment of Jack to the squadron seemed to close the door to his stepping up to the XO billet, so he was jubilant when Jack persuaded the skipper to let him step aside.

The only blot on Jeb Stuart's brief naval career was that he had spent some time as a "ploughback" after he got his wings. That is, after he was designated an aviator he was immediately turned around and made a flight instructor. Many good officers and aviators suffered that fate, but few were more incensed than Jeb Stuart. As a ploughback he was late getting into the war and he was determined to exploit his current cruise and job as "XO in a combat squadron" as a fast route to command before the war was over. He had seen enough of the Navy to recognize that a squadron command in combat would carry great weight in the peacetime Navy and would probably see him promoted eventually to Captain -- or higher if he played his cards right.

But Jeb Stuart had another reason for wanting to be the XO. He enjoyed the power it seemed to convey -- over the squadron's enlisted men and the junior pilots. He saw himself as the squadron disciplinarian and counselor -- "My job is to keep the skipper from getting involved in details." Jeb made the common mistake of confusing the office with real power. He had not yet learned that in a combat squadron (or almost any fleet unit for that matter) power is something that is conferred by the Navy, but can be exercised effectively only by an officer who has the respect and confidence of his subordinates. He confused his own false bonhomie and brisk peremptory manner with being accepted as a first among equals and wearing (deservedly in his view) the mantle of "command presence." His tour as XO was to be memorable -- both for him and his shipmates.

Jeb initially went out of his way to avoid antagonizing Jack. He even tried to butter Jack up, deferring in public to his undeniable combat experience and flight skills. But a sensitive ear would have picked up the innuendo that Jack "is different from you and me." In any event Jeb Stuart was not fitted for a deferential role when in fact (as he believed) he had the power to get his way. But matters progressed with no public disagreement between the two officers -- Jack had other things on his mind and Jeb found ample scope for his skills in squaring away the squadron's administration.

Jack's attempt to fade into the background in the air group came to naught because it turned out that he had more combat experience than any other pilot aboard and as many kills as the combined score of the veterans among the embarked fighter squadrons. Almost any question on fighter tactics saw Jack drawn into the discussion. He accepted this role with great reluctance, and a modesty that did not come naturally to him. He groaned inwardly when his seniors -- the CAG and the fighter squadron skippers --tried out some inane tactic on him. His patience was pressed to the breaking point when something "new and better" was suggested, an idea that had been shot down in blood in the Solomons.

As the task group in which USS President was one of four carriers sailed westward in the late spring of 1944, it was clear that a major amphibious operation was in the offing. By-passed Japanese islands in the Marshalls were clobbered by the task group for the practice it provided the green air crews. Losses were minimal and the air group was exuberant in the knowledge that they had been blooded and come out of the fight largely intact. Jeb Stuart had bagged a small Japanese float plane that had been caught airborne during a strike. He basked in the glow of accolades and in "taking the first step to becoming an ace." When he informed Jack that shooting down Japs was pretty simple in its basics, Jack just smiled and said that some Japs were tougher than others and that there would be ample opportunity to fight both kinds.

During his short time in the air group, Jack had been diligently scanning the various squadron "photo boards" and rosters to see if there was anyone on the ship who might have known Jack Dell or John Deal in an earlier incarnation. There was only one officer that fitted that description: "Snuffy" Purdom, a turkey pilot who might have gone through pre-flight and primary training with Jack when he was Jack Dell. Purdom sought Jack out and tried to strike up a reacquaintance one day as they were both going through the junior officer chow line. He noted the slight difference in Jack's name, and appeared to be satisfied when Jack told him that it was a mix up and that had been trying to get it corrected since pre-flight with no result. "It is easier to accept the Deal name than to continue fighting the bureaucracy." To which Purdom had responded,

"Bad enough that this damn Navy takes your freedom and maybe your life away without screwing around with your name."

Two weeks later this potential problem went away as Purdom was transferred to another air group to rebalance the effects of combat losses. In any event the names of old shipmates were not on anyone's mind as Task Force Fifty Eight -- and USS President -- were committed to support the invasion of the Mariannas and to be ready to take on the Japanese fleet that would surely respond to such a thrust.

And as predicted the Japanese did come out. Jack was launched one sunny morning in June as a division leader in a massive combat air patrol launch as many Japanese strike formations were reported inbound. Jeb Stuart led the other squadron division on the launch. Stuart made it clear during the pre-launch briefing in the squadron ready room that he considered himself in charge of both divisions even though such directive authority while airborne really belonged to the task group fighter director in the flagship's combat information center. Jack didn't contest Stuart's assertion because he knew that such rigid shipboard command lines did not mean anything once in the air. In short, he left Stuart's gaffe to the fighter director to square away.

The decks of the carriers in the task force had been cleared of dive bombers and torpedo planes (they flew to "lee side" of the task force to stay out of the way) so that the defending fighters could have the decks to themselves to land, refuel and rearm, and take off again -- in what the Navy called a "flex deck" operation. Stripped to its basics, the carriers provided "pit stops" for the busy fighters as a maximum effort was put into task group air defense.

Jack's and Jeb Stuart's divisions of four hellcats each were assigned high CAP to take on the Jap fighters accompanying the expected massive strike-- and if a suitable opportunity was presented they were to pick up Japanese bombers that had avoided other squadrons on CAP duty. It was a perfect day for a fight and the Japanese armada in staggered and stair-stepped lines of Vees proceeded majestically inbound to attack the Task Force. Jack quickly picked out the Jap fighters in this massive formation, but they showed no inclination to fight. The Japs apparently had been briefed to stay with the bombers. It was left to the HICAP to initiate action. Stuart and his division went in first -- their first encounter with Zekes. But they turned in too late, got sucked, and then to make up for it opened fire too soon with little result. They got one Zeke to show for their effort.

Jack's division followed quickly with just the right lead and spattered two Zekes on the first pass and then came up to get two more as the Japanese planes seemed more interested in staying out of the way and getting out alive than in protecting the bombers. The result was that after a few perfunctory efforts the Japs fled and Stuart's division pursued them in a long tail chase to the Western horizon. Jack found the air clear of fighters and requested and received permission from the fighter director to engage an overlooked incoming Jap raid of Kate torpedo bombers that had trailed the main strike. Before the fighter director could answer, Stuart tried to cancel the request saying he needed the assistance of Jack's division. As the fighter director and the XO tried to sort out where Jack's division was most needed, Jack headed for the incoming torpedo bombers and pushed over. The 12 Jap Kates were being held in a rigid "parade" formation. Jack's division fell on them in pairs and Jack flamed two of them on his first pass, and then got two more on his second pass while his wingman managed to get one. This continued for perhaps ten minutes and the entire Japanese flight was splashed.

It had been a slaughter of raw Japanese pilots tragically led by a rigid flight leader who didn't know how to cope with the slashing hellcats. As Jack pulled off and reported to the fighter director he mused that it had been their first -- and last -- fight. Short on fuel and with some planes out of ammo his division got in the President's landing pattern. After ten minutes on deck refueling and rearming they were launched again. The deck crew had seen nothing of the Stuart's division. Upon returning to station Jack was ordered to climb up and look for "leakers," stray Japanese aircraft that had escaped the clutches of the large and jubilant CAP.

Jack had never seen so many flaming aircraft in his life. The radio chatter indicated a field day in shooting down Japs. As the slaughter continued Jack saw three Kates homing in on the nearest U.S. task group. As he turned his division to port to dive on the leakers he thought of just how ticklish it would be to splash them without getting taken under fire by friendly but often undiscriminating anti-aircraft gun crews. On the way down to attack he was tempted to break Prather's rule and split up his flight to splash all the torpedo bombers on the first pass. But he held himself in check with a silent bow to the "old man" and they ended up shooting all three down anyway. It was the right decision because his inexperienced wingman would have pursued the Jap aircraft right down the Task Group's anti-aircraft gun barrels to get a kill. Good shooting by the lead aircraft in each section made such pressing unnecessary. The "slaughter of the innocents" continued and Jack got a Zeke and Kate before sunset and the retirement of the remnants of the Japanese air groups.

Back in USS President, the VF-277 ready room was a mad house as enthusiastic pilots laughed, hit each other on the back with mutual congratulations, and reenacted their victories. The air Intel officer had a difficult time getting the pilot debriefs in any coherent form. Jack was content to sit in his chair behind the CO, tilt it back, close his eyes in the tumult, and try to relax. That is until Jeb Stuart came storming in with fire in his eyes. His division had been the last to recover after flying only two sorties during that long day.

Jeb Stuart went up to Jack's chair and pulled him by the shoulder and shouted, "What the fuck do you think you were doing up there today, Deal? You broke flight discipline and went off to fight your own war. You ought to be grounded until you can learn to follow orders. I am personally going to debrief every member of your division to get their statements on all this. As it turned out, we about got our ass wiped by some returning Japs while you were whoring around with the easy pickings."

As this tirade continued, Jack looked up and with a vice like grip removed Stuart's hand from his shoulder. In a voice that was barely audible except to the startled skipper sitting directly in front of him, Jack said, "XO, if you have a beef with my flight performance, I suggest we adjourn to skipper's cabin and sort this out. In the meantime why don't you calm down, get a cup of coffee, and enjoy the feeling of being alive." At this point, the surprised skipper told his irate XO to "Stuff it, until we get a full debrief, review the gun camera results, and have a chance to calmly consider this fuckin' day."

With an effort at self control Stuart stormed stiff necked out of the ready room signaling the pilots in his division to follow him as he slammed the hatch open and departed. By 2100 that evening the results were clear: the famed "Mariannas Turkey Shoot" had gone into the history books. VF-277 had shot down 16 of the almost 450 Japanese planes shot down. Half of the squadron's sixteen had fallen to Jack's guns. The XO in his persistence had managed to shoot down one Japanese straggler. As he pursued the retreating Japanese fighters over the horizon, he had lost his wingman to a later returning wave of Japanese fighters.

The meeting with the CO that evening was stormy. Stuart insisted that Jack be grounded and put "in hack" (confined to his room) for "leaving his formation in the face of the enemy and pursuing personal glory at the expense of his squadron-mates." After fifteen minutes of this raging, the skipper put a stop to it by asking the XO what his flight's mission was. "Was it to shoot down Japanese bombers or go off haring after Japanese fighters trying to leave the fight?" Although a mild mannered man, his questions made it clear that it was the XO who had left the fight for personal glory and not Jack. During this tense session Jack kept calm only with great difficulty, answering the CO's and XO's questions dispassionately and paying no attention to the kill score attributed to him. They broke up with the Stuart gradually coming to realize he was on shaky ground in pursuing the matter further.

It made little difference because eight hours later the skipper was dead. His engine had quit during his catapult shot as he launched on the pre-dawn CAP. The ready room was stunned. It took just one hour for the XO to "take command." His first move after preparing the necessary death notifications and associated details of taking over was to call Jack to his cabin and inform him. "I am going to have your ass Deal, if you so much as look at me with anything other than respect. I think you are a glory seeking rat fucker who would sell us all down the river if it would give you one more kill."

Jack stood quietly and tried to see Gus Prather standing before him. But try as he might, Gus didn't appear. All he saw was a frightened, insecure SOB who would end up killing the squadron's pilots if he was let loose.

"Is that all, sir?"

"Yes, and get out of my sight!"

When Jack returned to the ready room, there was a message for him to report to the air group commander's office. A thousand thoughts went through Jack's mind on receiving this summons. Was it something about John Dell or Jack Deal? Had he received an inquiry from some would-be whistle blower? Did CAG believe he had screwed things up yesterday?

CAG McDowell was a burly man who had been a Naval Academy halfback ten years earlier and was now running to flesh. But he had a pair of cool eyes and an expression that conveyed a well developed sense of humor just beneath the surface of his rosy cherubic face.

"Sit down Deal. You had some day yesterday. It may just have set a record for one day's kill in this war. The Admiral and the Captain are excited as hell about it -- and we have received inquiries from Admiral Spruance's staff on the flagship. I want you to tell me about your day -- the way you saw it -- your part in it and the way our fighter employment was handled. You have more experience in the air fighting Japs than any of us and I want this air group to learn from your experience."

The dour face of Gus Prather began to take the place of CAG McDowell's happy Irish-American countenance as Jack reviewed the events of the day. He was careful but forthright in describing his difference of opinion with his XO. He matter of factly recounted the events of each firing run, stumbling only once or twice as he tried to remember actions that happened so fast there was no time to think about it. He ended his review with an opinion that the Japanese fighters were no longer a first rate enemy of the sort they had faced in the Solomons." They must be a bunch of kids right out of flight school and they are led by seniors of the old school who put more emphasis on discipline than on fight smarts. If they come out again, they're going to get another bloody nose."

CAG McDowell considered this extended explanation, and then said, "We lost a good man this morning in your CO. He was a personal friend. He wouldn't win any prizes as a dynamic leader. But in his own quiet way he was a dedicated fighter whose only regret would have been that he died in an operational accident and not in combat. He came to see me last night after he had debriefed you -- and your XO (this with a smile and rude snort) -- and said that he was putting you in for a medal for your day's work. Not just because you shot down eight Japs, but because you also made the right decisions in combat. You minded the store and did it well."

"I've got to find a replacement for him. I got three choices: Fleet up the XO (another snort), grab the XO of another squadron and put him in as your CO, or.......tell you to take over as acting skipper."

Jack started to get out of his chair but CAG brusquely waved him down. "Jack, you have bobbed and weaved long enough. I went along with the cockamamie idea of putting Jeb Stuart in the XO slot only because your skipper was an old friend. But he is gone and I am going to do my duty whether you like it or not." As he said the last CAG's jutting chin dared Jack to take exception to his decision.

"I have never seen a guy who was so born to fly yet is such a shrinking violet on deck. What are you hiding from? Don't you think you owe it to your guys to lead them rather than having Stuart do it? If you don't agree with that assessment, their blood could be on your hands! Enough! I am writing up a letter tonight directing you to take command as acting CO until Bupers can confirm it. My only concern is that you have the flag officers around here so "charmed" by their shrinking violet ace that they will grab you to serve on their staffs."

As Jack shuddered at the thought, McDowell said, "I thought that would get your attention. Now get your ass out of here -- skipper -- and teach that bunch of fuckers to fly as well as you do!"

When Jack returned to the squadron ready room, he told the duty officer "The skipper wants an all-pilots' meeting in the ready room at 0730 tomorrow morning. Pass the word."

* * *

At 0725 the next morning as the pilots gathered in the ready room, cups of coffee in their hands, Jack turned to the squadron duty officer and told him to tell "Lieutenant Stuart that the squadron pilots were assembled in the ready room."

Five minutes later Stuart stormed into the ready room asking who had called the meeting. Jack looked at him steadily and said, "I did. Please take a seat, XO. We've got lots to discuss."

As the XO started to protest Jack put his hand on his arm and gently pushed him into his chair across the aisle from him. He said quietly, "XO just hear this out and then you can say what you want."

Jack got up and looked at the pilots in the ready room. He made eye contact with each one, ending up with the XO. There was some throat clearing and foot shuffling as Jack pulled a piece of paper out of a lower pocket of his flight suit.

"I have been ordered to read this piece of paper to

you.

"From Lieutenant Commander Jacob McDowell USN, Commander Carrier Air Group Twenty Seven to Lieutenant John Deal USNR. Subject: orders. Upon receipt of this letter you are to relieve the current acting commanding officer of Fighter Squadron 277 and assume duties as acting commanding officer until relieved by competent authority."

Jack tossed the paper down on his chair and turned to the XO and said, "Mr. Stuart, will you please stand up?"

Stuart, beet red with embarrassment struggled to his feet as Jack said, "Mr. Stuart, I relieve you sir."

Stuart remained mute, finally asking, "May I see those orders -- sir?"

Jack gave them to him and after a few seconds accepted their return.

Jeb Stuart gave a smart salute with a bit of a smirk and said, "I stand relieved, sir." And then slumped in his chair. Jack then started to speak to his pilots. "We have a lot to mourn. We lost a fine skipper. But just as when your turn comes, the Navy will find someone to take your place as it has in this case. You all know I didn't seek this job -- in fact except for the fact I received a lawful order, I wouldn't have taken it. You didn't ask me to be your skipper but that makes us even; I didn't ask for you either. But somehow we will all make the best of it. As bad as it may be for you or me, it is better than getting a stranger in here to take over.

"I have only one comment on the big shootemup day before yesterday. Before you go feeling smug about what you and we did, I am here to tell you that you didn't face the Jap first team. Maybe they don't have a first team any more. But tell that to Skip Pennoyer who was shot down yesterday. Even a kid can shoot you down if you give him every chance to do so."

"Some of you are wondering what I plan to change. The answer is nothing except we are going to do some more talking about tactics -- so that the odds will be that you will do the right thing instead of the wrong thing. The XO (a nod towards Jeb Stuart) will continue to worry about administration and maintenance and I will worry about operations and tactics. Together we will lead and you will follow -- willingly or unwillingly -- your choice -- but you will follow until it is your turn to lead."

Turning to Stuart, he said, "XO, I would like to talk to the men this morning as soon as you can arrange it. Let me know when you have a time and a place set. That is all."

The next few days saw the Task Force continue in support of the invasion of Saipan and Tinian. The squadron was committed to fighter sweeps over the Mariannas airfields against a disorganized Jap force, many of whose planes were destroyed on the ground. It had become clear that the Japanese combined fleet had suffered a major defeat in what was being referred to as the Battle of the Philippines Sea.

One day some weeks later while the battle for Saipan reached its climax, Jack was summoned to CAG's stateroom and informed, "The staff has big plans for you. I know you won't like them but you don't stand a snowball's chance in hell of changing it, so if you fight them it will just make everyone's job harder to no good purpose. I will let them spell out the details. You've been a good shipmate and I hate to lose you. Good luck. And think of me: I have to put up with that bastard, Stuart!"

Rather than be apprised by a staff officer what all these mysterious plans were all about, Jack was ushered right into the Admiral's sea cabin and told to take a seat while awaiting the admiral.

Off to the right Jack heard a head flush and a few minutes later the Admiral came out wiping his hands on a paper towel. "Well, Deal I'm very pleased to meet you." Should have called you up to the bridge right away after your big day. Eight of those bastards in one day! I've never heard anything like it. Who taught you to shoot like that? The Admiral clearly wasn't looking for an answer but Jack gave him one anyway.

"Lieutenant Commander Gus Prather, sir. Best combat aviator I've ever seen."

"Hmmm, Prather you say....Can't say I've ever heard of him, but clearly we need more of his kind. But I didn't call you up here to talk about Prather. I want to talk about you. You are going to Pearl Harbor. Admiral Nimitz wants to see you, and I doubt you'll return to the fleet anytime soon."

"Sir, CAG told me it would be useless to protest these orders. I can see why if Admiral Nimitz wants to see me, but I hope you'll ask that I be returned to this ship after I see him. Going to Pearl Harbor is like being taken to the woodshed, with all due respect sir."

Jack, though sincere, wasn't perceptive enough to realize that his by now famous reticence merely whetted the appetites of his admirers: "Modest, doesn't seek any glory, just wants to kill Japs, utmost loyalty to his superiors, a fine lad -- wish we had more of them."

The Admiral laughed, "Woodshed or not -- that's a good one -- that's where you are bound. We are going to highline you off to a destroyer tomorrow morning and then its to Pearl by the next plane. Good luck, Deal. I envy you your achievements and your bright future. You are the example the home front is looking for!"

Jack pondered this last remark as he left the Admiral's sea cabin but put it down to a misplaced sense of Jack's role in the war.

* * *

Ten days later Jack was in Pearl Harbor, checked into CINCPAC headquarters at Makalapa as directed, and was told to cool his heels and have a good time in Honolulu until they could arrange a call on Admiral Nimitz. It was a classic Navy maneuver called, "Hurry up and Wait." Or its variant: "Pack the bags, unpack the bags." Except for a phone call to Maggie (the line to the phone booth in the lobby was at least one hundred yards long) the next week was miserable. Even the luxury of the stately Moana Hotel and plenty of liquor was insufficient to check his impatience. After a week of calling the staff each day to see when and if he was needed, he finally received some direction. He was to come to Admiral Nimitz's office at Makalapa at 1000 the next day in his best uniform.

As he was shown into the anteroom he saw a large crowd of officers gathered. He was given a glass of lemonade by the most attractive woman yeoman petty officer he had ever seen. Within minutes he was ushered into Admiral Nimitz's office and that tall husky gentleman strode forward to meet him. Jack was impressed by his suntan, his regular Teutonic features, and his piercing blue eyes. He grasped Jack's hand warmly, congratulating him on his performance off the Mariannas and telling him he was holding something for him. After a few moments chatting, and with the gathered staff officers laughing discretely at the Admiral's verbal sallies and Jack's embarrassment, the Admiral turned to his aide and told him it was time to get started.

The Admiral then turned to the group and said in his measured Texas drawl. "We are here this morning to honor an American fighting man. A man who has carried the banner with the fleet and brought it honor. A man who is a metaphor for all that is best in the American sailor...."

These kind words went on for a few minutes and then nodding to the aide Nimitz fell silent.

"The President of the United States takes great pleasure in awarding the Navy Cross, gold star in lieu of second award, to Lieutenant John Emerson Deal, United States Naval Reserve, for heroism and service as set forth in the following citation...."

Nimitz then pinned a Navy Cross on his wash khaki blouse, congratulated him, and after a few minutes of small talk ushered him out to the applause of the assembled officers. As Jack left the Chief of Staff beckoned Jack to one side and said "Follow me."

After they had settled in the Chief of Staff's office, that officer (who was a rear admiral) said, "Well, Deal I think your war is over. You are going to Washington to start a life of public appearances speaking for the War Bond drive."

Jack was appalled and looked frantically around for a way out of the room, this headquarters, this island, this war, and his deception. He felt as though his death sentence had been pronounced. It would be only a matter of days or weeks at the most before his true identity was revealed and his fraud exposed as the Navy publicity machine got into high gear.

"Are you all right, Deal? Most young officers I know would look forward to such an opportunity -- particularly if they had been through the various hells you have experienced in the last two years. If you are married, you will probably get to take your wife with you, if you are not you are likely to get more offers for company than any junior officer has a right to expect." The Admiral smiled at the prospect and clearly savored it for himself, wishing he were sitting across the table "instead of sitting on my fat butt in Pearl."

"Let me introduce Captain Lamb, the Staff Public Relations Officer. Your tail belongs to him now. He will get your program and your orders lined up starting with a press conference tomorrow morning."

* * *

The press conference was a disaster. While the reporters and photographers were interested in Jack's war exploits, they were more interested in his home town, where he went to school, who his teachers were, and all the minutia of John Dell's life that he had so valiantly tried to hide and forget. They pulled fact after fact out of him, occasionally tripping him up when he attempted a stupid evasion. Captain Lamb fumed that Jack was the "most difficult, fucked up hero I have ever encountered."

When it was over, Captain Lamb offered him some advice: "Relax and be forthcoming. You can't hide a damn thing from these bastards. You have the choice of enjoying the next six months or giving every public relations officer near you a nervous breakdown. If you play your cards right, you can feather your nest for when this war is over, but you can't do it if you play cute."

Lamb continued, "Nimitz wanted you to get the Congressional Medal of Honor for what you did, but he doesn't have authority to award it. All those recommendations have to be approved by Washington, but he intends to pursue it. You are going to really embarrass the old man if you continue this stupid 'little ole me, don't mess with my privacy' act!"

Lamb handed him his orders on the flight out the next morning. Jack approached the next few days with a terror that he had never experienced before. The only good news he could see was that he would soon be with Maggie again. But could their marriage stand the winds of the storm that was brewing? It was with a heavy heart that he boarded the C-54 transport at Hickham Field the next morning.

Chapter 7 - Fugitive

The crowded Skymaster had been flying all night and the sun was just rising over the Sierra as it crossed the California coastline and proceeded on to March Field near San Bernardino. In some ways the flight for Jack had been similar to the one he had taken the previous December as he came back to the States from Tavabatu. On that occasion he was worried about confronting Maggie Fitzgibbons with his deception. This time he was confronting the need to shed his John Deal identity and become someone else. As he thought about his options he took out a packet in his B-4 bag containing all his records as Jack Dell: pay record (allotment to Maggie), health record (no war wound recorded), service record (the clock stopped the day he left Maui more than a year earlier), and his flight log book (with only some 410 flight hours in it).

Picking up as Jack Dell after a year would be ticklish business. Some alteration of the record would be needed if he were to become Jack Dell again. Where had he spent the last year? Should he carry out Jack Dell's original orders back to Pensacola and fill in the blanks somehow? Was anybody out looking for Jack Dell?

As he thought about it, a plan began to form in his mind. He would again become Jack Dell but would borrow a page or two from John Deal's service record. He would alter the name to show that Jack Dell had gone to VF-241 at Tavabatu at the same time that "John Deal" had gone there. Then instead of being the John Deal who left Tavabatu wounded, he would be Jack Dell who left VF-

241 at the same time but reported to the CINCPAC staff at Pearl Harbor as one of several staff pilots. He already had a CINCPAC set of orders that he could alter to send him on to Pensacola. He would need a typewriter and some "white out" to make the alterations, but that could await his arrival in the States. First, John Deal had to disappear. It was too late to get him off the passenger manifest for this flight. He would have to disappear on arrival at March Field. And somehow he would have to call Maggie............

After the plane landed he had a near miss in avoiding reporters waiting for him at base operations. He managed to dodge going to operations by cadging a ride at plane-side on a mini-bus designated for a group of senior officers being chauffeured to LA. Their plans included partying a while before going on to carry out their orders. They happily took him along as a mascot. There was much macho talk of liquor to be drunk and ladies to be "entertained" before getting on once again with the war. But once in LA, Jack quickly left the revelers behind and went to a phone booth to call Maggie.

Before dropping in the coins, Jack took a deep breath. How about ditching Maggie too? Go solo? It would be tougher including her, but dammit! He loved that crazy girl. They had both finally leveled with each other. If he ditched her now, he could never return. He decided he needed her help and support, and was willing to pay the price in complications that would inevitably ensue.

He dialed the number and dropped in the requisite coins. A sleepy Maggie answered the phone. Johnny was crying in the background.

"Maggie? Jack. Listen closely. I can only talk for a few minutes. Unfortunately I have become something of a hero and you will be getting calls from the Navy and reporters asking questions and wondering where John Deal is. My time as John Deal is up and I am becoming Jack Dell again...

"But Jack where are you? Are you home? When can I see you?...."

"Honey, no time for that now. I am going to give you a set of instructions. Don't write them down. Just memorize them!"

"Oh, God. We've got to be the craziest bunch of fugitives anyone ever heard of. But, OK, I'm listening."

"First, when the Navy or reporters come calling, just tell them the truth. Your husband John Deal is in VF-277 on an aircraft carrier. But that you haven't heard from him in recent weeks."

"Second, if they ask if you have talked to him since he returned to the States, just say you don't know what they're talking about. Stick with that story regardless."

"Third, in three months leave the apartment with whatever you and Johnny need to travel and go to Pensacola, Florida. Pay all your bills and do not leave a forwarding address. Cover all your tracks. Meet me in the Lobby of the San Carlos Hotel on your birthday the 20th of November at 6 PM.I say again: The lobby of the San Carlos on your birthday at 6 PM. Tell no one where you are going or why. You should have enough money in your checking account to make the trip. I will make all arrangements to meet you in Pensacola as Lieutenant Jack

Dell. This will be a bitch because the Navy and the reporters will be tough as hell. Any questions, Maggie?"

"No, Jack, I will see you on my birthday. I love you and hope we can stop running some day." This last was accompanied by a sob.

"I love you too, honey. This war won't last forever, and then we can leave the Navy and the lies behind us. For now just think of what we are going to do in that room in the San Carlos. Good-bye, Maggie. Love you."

As he put the receiver down, Jack saw something different before his eyes. It was a goddam tear going down his cheek. "Shit, I haven't cried since I was five years old when my old man beat the hell out of me."

Jack spent the rest of the day in LA at the downtown USO using a borrowed typewriter to start fixing up his Jack Dell service record. He then caught a ride to the Naval Air Station at Los Alamitos where he tried out his new identity by getting his back pay as Jack Dell and visiting the personnel office over the lunch hour to pick up some personnel record forms he needed. He quickly promoted himself to lieutenant junior grade and lieutenant in his updated service record. He knew Gus Prather wouldn't mind granting him these well deserved promotions. The transactions were helped by the fact that the personnel office supervisors were out to lunch leaving in charge a sleepy yeoman striker who liked to gab. That night he bunked at the BOQ and hitchhiked a flight out the next morning to Corpus Christi. Jack Dell was on his way....

Lieutenant Jack Dell USNR reported to the personnel office of Naval Air Station Pensacola, Florida on the 25th of August 1944 for further assignment. John Deal's and Jack Dell's few friends would not have recognized him. He had a very close-cropped haircut complemented by a substantial mustache. Because it turned down at the corners of his upper lip, his face seemed to have a sorrowful expression, little relieved by his apparent inability to smile. He wore an ill-fitting wash gray uniform -- Admiral Ernie King's unwanted gift to the Navy officer corps. He wore his Tavabatu ribbons, but not the Navy Cross ribbon with the gold star. His posture was slouched and unmilitary. To a regular officer who might observe him he projected an image of the worst characteristics of the war-service only reservist.

As Jack entered the personnel office in one of the rundown Civil War era buildings in use at that old naval establishment, he knew he was embarking on a crap shoot. He was well aware that it wouldn't take much to penetrate his renewed identity as Jack Dell. He also knew that he would enter a lottery for assignment to any of a large number of unwanted jobs in the large air training command centered around Pensacola and its many satellite training fields. He has already resigned himself to not getting back into flying status, even though his flight log book had been "brought up to date" to reflect his flying hours with VF-241 at Tavabatu. But his first hurdle was to get by the officer who ran the personnel office.

Chief Warrant Officer Sylvester Yates was no Chief "Putty" Benson. He was a small gimlet eyed man who seemed at first impression to run an efficient office whose products were tidy records, matching bodies with billets, and keeping a large number of transiting officers moving smartly into and out of the command. He was a reservist who had been an office manager of a small insurance company before the war. When Jack reported in, Yates went over his service record page by page, often stopping to flip back and forth between pages as though trying to understand the sequence of assignments recorded therein. When he looked up he said,

"Lieutenant, this is the most fucked up record and set of orders I have ever seen -- and I thought I had seen them all. Let me see if I have this straight. You had orders back here a year ago from VF-321 -- they were at NAS Lahaina, right? Then you were ordered on temporary duty to VF-241 somewhere in the south Pacific before you were detached last winter and ordered to the staff of CINCPAC in Hawaii. Then someone on that dung pile got tired of you and had you carry out your original orders back here to Pensacola. I have heard that there is a war on (this with a contented grin as he looked out his window at the calm green waters of a serene Pensacola Bay), but this is ridiculous. You got anything to say about this goddam run-around?"

"Nope,' Just go where they tell me. But sure is good to be back in the States. Not much ass in the Solomons -- or Hawaii either for that matter."

Not to be distracted, Yates bored in, "What I don't understand, Lieutenant, is not why they sent you to VF-241, but why they ordered you back here in the first place.

Did you screw up out in beautiful Maui -- or in the Solomons? If those guys in VF-241 weren't fighting the war, I sure as hell would ask them what was going on."

Yates paused for a moment and thumbed through a large loose-leaf book. "Shit, I see that VF-321 got decommissioned last spring. No help there. Well hell, you're here and we've got to put you somewhere. The powers that be just cut back the pilot training rate. Some smart bastard has probably figured out that the Japs have lost the war -- probably the same bastard that sent you here. Well I can tell you that even though Commander Aldrich will make your assignment here, you really only have two choices: test pilot at the overhaul and repair hangar here at the Naval Air Station, or officer in charge of the station's crash boats on the waterfront. You won't make admiral out of either one, but if it was me I would take the crash boat job and get some fishin' in. What'll it be?" Jack thought quickly about which job would be most out of sight. The test pilot job would put him in contact with all sorts of pilots testing or ferrying aircraft -- and some of them might recognize either John Deal or Jack Dell. Most pilots wanted nothing to do with ground or sea jobs like running crash boats.

Smiling, Jack said, "Well Mr. Yates, I'll take your advice. I need to do some fishing anyway."

That evening Jack looked into the BOQ bar and quickly withdrew. There were two officers in a booth with a row of empty glasses lined up on the table. Both looked familiar to Jack -- either VF-321 or VF-241, or maybe......"I've got to get out of this place." The next morning he arranged to get permission to live off-base and get a housing allowance. Before sundown he was settled in a small rented bungalow in the back yard of a larger house in Warrington, just outside the main gate of the Naval Air Station. It cost more than he could really afford, but he had little choice. Besides, in November he had to have a place for Maggie and Johnny.

Two days later Jack walked into his job as the officer-in-charge of crash boats at the Naval Air Station. His office was in a small shed adjacent to the piers. His "command" consisted of three 60 foot crash boats for the rescue of downed airmen and 25 enlisted men headed up by a warrant bosun who was rarely around. The scuttlebutt was that "Boats" showed up every two weeks for his paycheck and a boat ride around the bay. Jack's boss was the Station Operations Officer who had absolutely no interest in the crash boats and their crews except demanding that they fish the stray student aviator out of the Gulf.

With the Bosun rarely around the enlisted crews and their scheduling were run by a first class quartermaster. A big burly old salt of the pre-war Navy, he knew exactly how much he could get away with and how little attention he could pay to officers. When Jack showed up to take charge, Petty Officer "Warts" Wartburg could be heard muttering "fuckin' aviators."

He asked Jack if he wanted a cup of coffee and then sat down and proceeded to tell him "You stay outta my way, and I stay outta yours, OK? -- Sir?" Jack responded by giving him the full Prather treatment: an emotionless stare, looking Warburg over, then standing up and walking around the shed, saying nothing but pulling out desk drawers and looking inside. After about five minutes of this silent treatment, Wartburg stood up, stretched, and said, "Well, if you ain't got anything to talk about, I'll get on with our work, Lieutenant."

Jack turned to face him, growling, "Set your fuckin ass back down. I got news for you. First, I don't like your name -- so I'm going to call you 'chief.' Even though you ain't one, you sure act like one. You do things my way and you may even get a chief's hat before this war is over.

"Second, I want you to muster the crews -- all that aren't out in the Gulf -- so I can talk to them. If you gave them the afternoon off, get'em in here drunk or sober tomorrow morning at 0630. Third, I want to see the boats this afternoon. I want you to give this 'fuckin aviator' a special tour of your little fleet. Every nook and cranny. I'll tell you now that if I find a single bottle of hooch in the boats, you are fired this afternoon. Just to show you I'm not unreasonable, I'll give you a half hour to get the boats ready for inspection.

"Fourth, I don't know a rat's ass from a crash boat -- but I'm a fast fuckin learner. My bullshit meter will tell me in a minute whether I'm being conned. If you try to con me one more time I will break your goddam face! Got that, Chief? OK, your thirty minutes starts now. Move it!"

This gentle but frank conversation kicked off a productive and mutually respectful relationship between "Chief" Wartburg and Jack. Within two months the crash crews were squared away and Jack was left alone by the air station hierarchy. Jack's sailors were even proud of their "one tough sonnabitch" skipper. There was only one embarrassment: One crash crew covered itself with glory picking up three aviators from the Gulf in a single day during bad weather. The resulting publicity had Jack ducking to stay out of the camera's eye.

As he turned his calendar to November Jack began to feel the excitement building in him. He wondered if Maggie would come, or whether she had cut her losses and stayed married to the missing John Deal. Since no one had apparently come looking for him in Pensacola, he hoped that she had honored their bargain. He didn't dare telephone her because he didn't know anything about phone taps on her line. All it would take was a whiff of information that the missing John Deal was in Pensacola to have Navy intelligence and reporters on his case.

On November 20th he told "Chief" Wartburg that he was taking the rest of the day off to do some things around the house. From then on time seemed to stop and he waited for the clock to get into afternoon. He was tempted to have a couple of drinks, but called on his reserves of will power to put the bottle away. At five o'clock he was in the lobby of the San Carlos and started his vigil. Six o'clock came and went. Finally at six twenty a taxi pulled up at the hotel and a harassed Maggie got out with a screaming Johnny. He caught the taxi driver before he pulled away and had him take them "home." During the drive they sat in the taxi without saying a word, as Johnny gradually settled down and eventually went to sleep in

Jack's arms.

Closing the door to their cottage, Maggie flew into Jack's arms and sobbed. "Oh, Jack, these past three months have been hell! I didn't know there were so many bastards in the world. I've been called names, called at all hours of the night, been followed, had my mail opened, and had cops at my door nearly every week."

"Maggie, I want to hear every detail -- later. For now I am so glad you are home. I love you. You are one tough broad -- and I love every inch of your gorgeous body. No matter what happens to us in the future, I will always remember your guts and love. Now, we have to move quickly while Johnny is still asleep....

Chapter 8 - Reckoning

Jack and Maggie kept to themselves in Pensacola. Jack had stopped his Jack Dell pay allotment to Maggie and as far as the Navy knew now, he was a bachelor officer living in town. Some curious brother officers knew he kept a girl and her child in his house. But Jack warded off inquiries as to his marital status and turned down most social invitations. In spite of these vestiges of their fugitive existence Jack and Maggie experienced fully the joys of being together and of married life. But a week after VJ Day in August 1945 their lives began unraveling. It started with Jack's receiving a call to stop by the air station legal office. He stiffened when he received the summons. But even if it turned out to be the worst, he knew his days of running were over. He would fight exposure, but he wouldn't run from it. He knew the only thing in his favor was that he was in fact Jack Dell and not John Deal.

The legal officer was Commander Sean Murphy, a portly, seemingly jolly reservist who had to leave his lucrative Boston legal practice when he was called up after Pearl Harbor. But if one looked closely into Murphy's eyes one saw the sharp eyes of a no-holds-barred expensive trial attorney. Jack was determined not to be cocky or to underestimate Commander Murphy.

Murphy welcomed Jack, had the yeoman fetch him a cup of coffee, and engaged in small talk about crash boats for about five minutes before swinging around in his swivel chair and fixing Jack with his direct blue eyes.

"Lieutenant, the Captain has received information

from a source that I cannot identify that suggests that you may not be Jack Dell, but someone called John Deal. It seems someone believes you may be masquerading as another man. Anything to say about that?"

Jack was ready for a charge that he had impersonated John Deal, but not for an allegation that he was not in fact Jack Dell. It was though the tables had not only been turned around, but that they had been turned upside down. It astounded him that some Navy snoops considered John Deal more real than Jack Dell. It was testimony to the effectiveness of his impersonation of John Deal. In spite of his surprise Jack found a ready reply.

"Commander, it ought to be an easy matter to check with Washington to see if my ID and fingerprints match those of this John Deal. Are you testing me or playing games, sir? You didn't call me up here to ask me a question that could be irrefutably answered by the Bureau of Naval Personnel. What gives?"

"Whoa, Lieutenant, this isn't a court of law. I've received an inquiry from people whose duty it is to ask questions and to establish the truth when it is of interest to the Navy. Are you telling me that this is simply a case of mistaken identity?"

"Sir, I can't rightly say what your informants are up to and what information they have. All I know is that I am Jack Dell. And there are ample records to back it up. Is it really so hard to get the facts sir?"

"Well, someone has good reason to believe you are a guy named John Deal, a war hero who returned to the States last year and mysteriously disappeared -- just before you showed up in Pensacola. Did you ever know or meet a John Deal?"

"Well there was a John Deal in the Solomons the same time I was, but I didn't know him well. Last year we did a lot of shuffling around from field to field and I think Deal may have left before I did. He could be the same Deal you say disappeared."

"Clearly the folks who have relayed their information to me have more work to do. I am surprised they haven't already checked you out with Washington. I agree with you, it should be a simple matter to compare your identification with the records in DC. I was hoping to get this wrapped up today and tell the skipper to forget about it. But can you think of any reason a person would think you were John Deal?"

"No sir, except we served in the same combat area and it is possible that our names are not far apart in how they are spelled."

Murphy sat appraising Jack for several seconds and then sighed. "Deal is either dead or AWOL and has been for a year. If he is dead we will want to find out more about how he died. If he is still alive, he's got to face the music on a desertion charge, war hero or not. That's all, Dell, I suspect we will be talking some more when we have more facts. Good day, sir."

As Jack reached the door, Murphy barked, "Deal, come back here for a moment...."Jack froze, but refused to turn around, except gradually to face Murphy."

"Commander, you are a hard fucking loser -- with your cheap courtroom tricks. I thought I made it clear that you are talking to Lieutenant Jack Dell, sir. If you feel otherwise, get your evidence together and get the charges sworn to."

Murphy wasn't the least embarrassed by being caught out." Dell, you sound like a guy who has faced charges before. Very touchy aren't we? Well while we are looking up Jack Dell in DC, we'll also see if he has ever appeared before a court martial. Good day, Mr. Dell."

And there matters remained for some weeks until Jack was again summoned to the air station legal office. But instead of seeing Murphy, he was ushered into a nearly bare cubicle of an office and introduced to a Mr. David Weymouth. Weymouth as a short thin man with regular features and curly blond hair. He was dressed in a cheap light blue suit worn over a lemon yellow shirt that he had sweat through in the late summer heat. His most disconcerting feature was a baleful stare that seemed to penetrate right to the core of the person being interrogated.

He used the stare on Jack but had no way of knowing that Jack had learned how to handle a stare from an expert. So, it was for a full two minutes that David Weymouth and Gus Prather's star pupil stared at one another. In the end Jack began to smile and asked Weymouth,

"Where did you serve in the war, Mr. Weymouth? You look fit enough to me."

"Lieutenant Dell, it is my job to ask the questions and it is your job to answer them. I don't need your wise-ass remarks about my personal history. I am here to check some facts about your background. And I will warn you I already know a lot, so it will be to your benefit to level with me."

Jack considered this reply for several seconds. Weymouth was the type of questioner who tried to intimidate his witnesses and bluff that he held all the cards. Jack decided to send the ball flying back into Weymouth's court and play his own intimidation game.

"No need to get touchy. But you misunderstand our positions. I want to know the point of your questions before I answer any of them. A couple of weeks ago I went through a bunch of bullshit in this office, and before I go through anymore with you I want to know who you are and where you are coming from. How do I know you are David Weymouth? Show me your authority to ask me questions and my obligation to answer them."

Weymouth reddened under these words and brought out his wallet with an ID Card that stated that the bearer was Special Agent David Weymouth of the Investigations Branch of the Office of Naval Intelligence. Jack looked at it slowly reading every word and then turned it over and did the same. When he was finished he returned the card and dug out his own ID card and pushed it over to Weymouth.

"Mr. Weymouth, would you please read the name on that card and see if it tallies with the picture on it -- fingerprints too if you want."

Weymouth brushed the card away with a snarl, "I already know who you claim to be. That is why I am here."

"Mr. Weymouth, I resent your insinuating I am not who I claim to be while insisting that you are who you claim to be. I refuse to answer any more questions unless you get a witness in here. I find your conduct unprofessional. Show me the proof that I am not Jack Dell. If you cannot produce that proof, I am going to report you to my commanding officer for harassment and making false official statements." Jack started to get up when Weymouth slumped in his chair while waiving Jack to sit down.

But Jack didn't let up. "Tell me how many Japs you have killed with your silly-assed questions, Mr. Weymouth. I think you spent the war flashing your ID and kicking little old ladies.....

Finally, Weymouth held up his hand and said wearily, "Lieutenant, what do you say we start all over again and forget everything that has been said or implied to this point? I have a job to do, not as demanding or as glamorous as the job your record says you did in the Pacific, but a job just the same. Let's just forget witnesses and playing games. To demonstrate my good faith, I am going to tell you why I am here and why I asked to see you."

"You are not accused of anything. I am only trying to establish a set of facts that may explain the disappearance of Lieutenant John Deal a year ago. We simply don't know where he is. Not only that, his wife doesn't know what happened to him. He simply vanished into thin air. You have been identified by a reporter, I can't tell you who or how, as looking very much like the John

Deal he saw in Pearl Harbor last year when John Deal received the Navy Cross."

"This is not a court of law and I am not a prosecutor. I am an employee of the Navy Department just as you are. Your job (looking at Jack's wings) is to fly planes, my job is to ask questions and establish facts. Some of these facts may someday lead to criminal prosecution of parties unnamed at this point. If you refuse to answer my questions you can be charged with obstruction of an official investigation. Now, can we proceed without muddying the waters any more?"

Jack nodded. "I apologize Mr. Weymouth. I get pissed off when people -- you or Commander Murphy -- question who I am all because a reporter thinks he sees a resemblance. Why don't you tell me more about what you know about Lieutenant John Deal? As I told Commander Murphy some weeks ago, I barely knew a John Deal in the Pacific. Obviously he has been up to no good since I last saw him or you wouldn't be trying to trace him."

"Lieutenant, you are still playing games with me. I don't have to tell you a damn thing. I have information I don't have to share with you. I am the one who is getting information, not you."

"Mr. Weymouth, with all due respect, I submit that you are the one playing games with me. You are holding information, apparently looking for some error of recollection on my part that you can use to make some larger point that is unknown to me. Why don't you simply tell me what you know about John Deal and when and how he disappeared. Maybe I can help with what little I know about him."

Clearly exasperated, Weymouth said, "All right, you fucking sea lawyer. John Deal was from Canoga Park, California, went through flight training in 1942 and early 1943. He reported to VF-321 at NAS Lahaina in the Hawaiian Islands in the spring of 1943. There things get kind of fuzzy. Some people say he was killed in an aviation accident. There is even a handwritten record of an aircraft accident investigation endorsed by a Commander named Jake Womble, said Commander Womble is now in a medical institution and out of his mind. But other evidence shows that John Deal was alive enough to go on and report to VF-241 in the Solomons. Unfortunately, VF-241 was decommissioned about the time you left and we haven't been able to track down the squadron records. Along the way John Deal picked up two Navy Crosses."

Jack scratched his head and looked at a spot two feet over Weymouth's head. "All I remember of Deal is that he seemed to shoot down a lot of Japs. His Navy Cross, er Crosses, is news to me. I remember him as a loner, but hell, I was too. He probably couldn't tell you anything more about me than I can tell you about him."

After a pause, Jack continued, "Are you just looking for one AWOL war hero, or is there something else bothering this fucking Navy system?"

"Being AWOL is bad enough, but this 'fucking Navy system' as you call it hates a mystery. Why would a war hero disappear suddenly? All the witnesses that could identify the real John Deal, assuming you aren't him, are either dead or scattered to the four winds. The records are either all fucked up or don't exist."

"Well, Mr. Weymouth, my guess is that Mr. John fucking Deal has something to hide. If he isn't dead -- or even if he is -- he must have been running from something. Maybe he ran off with the squadron payroll, maybe he screwed the skipper's wife, maybe he ran up some gambling debts, maybe someone wants his ass about something personal, maybe he was found in bed with a queer. All I know is that I don't give a shit about John Deal's problems. I am Jack Dell and I can prove it -- and you know it. So why don't you look for some old ladies to pick on instead of playing mind games with me on a hot summer day in Pensacola? We've both got better things to do."

"I will check up on you Lieutenant Jack Dell. I have a hunch I can't prove now that you are holding out on me. Why, I don't know --yet. And one more thing: Don't think that just because you are returning to civilian life now that the war is over and all that we can't put an arm on you. There are federal offenses involved in this story. If you are hiding anything, it would be better to come clean while you are on active duty. You can continue to draw your Navy pay, get a Navy lawyer, and cry on the shoulder of your CO while you see through whatever it is that comes of all this. Once you are a civilian you could end up in the clink until we get all the facts, and face a steely eyed federal judge rather than a sympathetic court martial, Think it over wise guy. You'll be seeing me again."

In spite of his bluster, Jack left the office shaken. He looked at the threat and the state of his defenses. The threat was in several dimensions. Sooner or later Weymouth or someone like him would examine and compare the pay and health records of John Deal and Jack Dell. They would see that John Deal had not drawn any pay for two years and that Jack Dell had contrived to have his allotment sent to his bank. Later they would see that for a while he had a pay allotment made out to a Mrs. Jack Dell. They might see that John Deal had spent some time in a Navy hospital for surgery to his leg, even though his health record was unaccountably missing. It would be a simple matter to ask to see his leg, find out where he lived, identify Maggie as in fact Mrs. John Deal, and so on until the whole house of cards collapsed.

As if these fears were not enough, it wouldn't be long before someone else mistook him for John Deal and the whole dreadful business would start all over again. His discharge date was still at least sixty days away, not enough time to keep the Murphy's, Weymouth's, and others like them at bay. He seemed to have two choices: continue to fight, deceive, bob and weave and hope he could get discharged and disappear before the roof caved in -- or he could confess all and hope that his combat record would keep him out of the Navy's prison at Portsmouth. He had been successful in staying out of sight in Pensacola except for one damning moment when one of his best crash boat crews had received awards -- well photographed by the local news media -- for their daring rescue of a downed pilot in the Gulf. Jack apparently had not managed to stay out of the photographs.

He could send Maggie away to counter one

vulnerability. As Jack Dell he was not married -- except for that brief period when he had sent her a pay allotment. But he couldn't bear the thought of putting Maggie and Johnny on the road again after what they had been through.

That night Maggie and Jack reviewed the situation after dinner. It was a long evening, one that continued well into the night. Eventually, after many tears they agreed that their best course of action was to clear up the deception while they still held some cards. So it was with a heavy heart that Jack called on Commander Murphy the next morning.

Murphy eyed Jack warily as he entered his office. "You here to complain about Weymouth? If you are, you're wasting your breath and my time. He's doing his job like he's supposed to. And you are supposed to be helping him not working him over. What's on your mind?"

"Sir, I need an attorney. I have some information on Lieutenant John Deal and some of it could be self-incriminating. I will cooperate with the Navy investigation about Deal's disappearance, but I need an attorney to advise me as to how to proceed without putting myself in unnecessary jeopardy."

Murphy's entire demeanor changed. From his impatient, wary, but relaxed attitude he shifted to a businesslike and formal manner. "Dell, you don't have a right to a Navy attorney unless you are officially accused of an offense against Navy laws and regulations. Instead you have an obligation to cooperate fully with any official investigation. Are you telling me you will not cooperate because of possible self incrimination?"

"Yes sir. I have information that is potentially self incriminating and I am asking for legal counsel before answering any further questions about Lieutenant John Deal."

Murphy sat back in his chair and pursed his lips. "I could tell you to go to hell, Dell, and have Weymouth proceed and if charges were brought against you as an accessory to Deal's disappearance, we could handle the counsel issue at that time. You really don't hold any cards in this matter."

"I understand, sir. I don't have anything to gain by saying anything -- and I potentially have a lot to lose. I will retain a civilian attorney if the Navy can't provide one."

Murphy didn't like that one bit. There were already rumbles in the Navy legal community that civilian lawyers were taking up veterans' cases where there were alleged injustices while their clients were on active duty. The post-war backlash against military justice had already begun. He didn't want a civilian attorney nosing around in Navy matters -- particularly in this situation with the prospect of a lot of dirty laundry and publicity in a case that would likely have high public interest. But he had only a half dozen judge advocate corps officers and they were kept busy running the air station's trial machinery.

But as Jack got up to leave Murphy saw an out. He had a newly assigned officer on his staff who had not been aboard long enough to find his way around the Navy legal system. He would let him cut his teeth on representing Dell.

"OK, Dell, I will assign an attorney to advise you

as you cooperate with the investigative authorities. But bear in mind that attorney works for the base CO as I do. He can advise you but he is not a defense counsel because as yet no charges have been made or are under considerations. Are we agreed?"

"I think so, sir. Can you hold Weymouth off long enough to let me consult with my attorney, who is...?"

"His name is Lieutenant junior grade Abraham Smith. Show up here tomorrow morning ready to discuss this matter with him and be prepared to meet with Weymouth tomorrow afternoon."

The next morning Jack again presented himself at the legal office and was taken down the hall to Lt. J.G. Smith's office. The escorting sailor knocked and was told to enter. Jack was left to open the door.

Behind the desk in the small office was the largest, blackest naval officer Jack had ever seen -- which wasn't saying a great deal because there were few black officers, much less JAG corps officers, in the United States Navy of late 1945. A deep voice boomed out, "Well, Lieutenant haven't you ever seen a nigger lawyer before? Come on in and tell me all about the load of shit you and I have to clean up together. Let me say right off that I consider this just another shitty detail in a Navy full of shitty details. The Navy doesn't like the idea of a Nigra officer -- certainly no Nigra lawyers that might make trouble on this plantation! I didn't ask for this job, but they have to keep me busy -- and you are my very first case."

Jack was appalled. Murphy had palmed him off on

a black legal officer who by all indications hadn't been in the Navy six months. So much for getting good legal advice. But he knew he had to make the best of it -- and he felt an instant bond with this pissed off officer who had already been pushed around by the system. So Jack threw the dice and decided to play the hand the Navy had dealt him.

"If you don't mind, I will call you Abe. My name is Jack Dell. Why don't we start by shaking hands. I will tell you I've never met a Negro naval officer before, but that I'm from Oregon and up there we only care how good a guy is and we don't care much about his color -- even though other folks seem to worry a lot about it."

"I've got a story to tell you Abe, but first of all I need to know whether you are my attorney and I am you client -- or whether you are just another motherfucker like Murphy but in a different package."

Abe Smith laughed long and hard at this. "So you don't like him either -- Well, he doesn't get paid to be liked. As to whether I am your attorney, it depends on what you have done or not done. If you have committed a crime, I am duty bound to report it to the Navy command authorities. I cannot conceal or withhold evidence in any official investigation or legal proceedings. Other than that I am in your corner, your advisor -- and maybe even a friend. But I should tell you I barely got through Howard Law School. I have a keen nose for justice as well as the law -- and they aren't necessarily the same thing. The law enslaved my people for two centuries but justice set them free. With that little speech, I am Lieutenant junior grade

Abraham Lincoln Smith, Judge Advocate General Corps, United States Naval Reserve at your service."

As Abe held out his hand he continued, "All I know about this is that Commander Murphy believes you may be someone else, or at least may know something about the mysterious disappearance of that someone else about a year ago. Apparently, there are two actors in this tragedy: a John Deal and a Jack Dell. Which one are you?"

"Both. What I am going to tell you is the truth -- even if it sounds unbelievable. I am in fact Jack Dell, but for about a year I masqueraded as John Deal. That masquerade ended about a year ago when I resumed my real identity as Jack Dell."

"I changed my identity with a little good luck -- and some connivance -- from Jack Dell to John Deal in the summer of 1943 while Deal and I were assigned to VF-321 at NAS Lahaina on Maui. I had just been court martialed for assault and other 'high crimes and misdemeanors' and was being sent back home -- to Pensacola -- in disgrace. The day I was to leave VF-321 John Deal was killed in a stupid air accident. I was ordered to inventory his personal effects before I left -- another shit detail -- and saw how easy it would be to take his place. Because of sloppy administrative procedures and safeguards in VF-321 carrying out Deal's orders to VF-241 in the South Pacific wasn't hard."

Jack continued his description of his last day in VF-321 and how he had carried out the deception in which John Deal received a new life. During this description Abe Smith nodded and even smiled. At one point he even laughed outright.

"You are one smart motherfucker. You really screwed the system good. Hell you shoulda been in Washington DC where I grew up. We could have used your smarts and balls in my little group of friends. Most of 'em need a lawyer worse than you do."

Jack continued the story through his tour in VF-241, his wounding, recovery, and later assignment to VF-277 in the President. He didn't talk about his combat record -- only that he had been there and done his job. But Abe Smith wouldn't let him skip past that.

"Ever shoot down any Japs?"

"Yes."

"How many?"

"Eighteen that the Navy knows about. But there may have been a half dozen more."

"Woweeeee! You are a real killer. A real fuckin hero! They give you any medals?

"Yeah, a lot of them including two Navy Crosses."

"So John Deal got the medals but Jack Dell got the experience. That right?"

"Yeah, but being John Deal, hero and all, was no bed of roses. I'm glad he is dead and buried."

"What pushed you over the rim to shuck Deal's identity and go into hiding, showing up here to be Jack Dell again?"

"After I got the second Navy Cross, there was a lot of publicity -- press conferences, photos, being told I was going to be part of a touring group promoting war bonds, all that stuff. Then one of the officers on Admiral Nimitz's staff said the Admiral was going to put me in for the Medal of Honor -- and that broke it. When I flew into the States, I shucked John Deal and became Jack Dell again. I had to do a little creative paperwork to fill in the gaps, but it was good enough to get me here and keep folks from bothering me for a year."

"I'm interested in this girlfriend of John Deal. You say you married her. How the hell did you carry that off. Didn't she love the guy? What'd she say when you showed up instead of her one true love?"

Jack went through his correspondence with Maggie, their mail order marriage, how he had confronted her with the truth, their trouble in putting the past behind them and starting a life together, the questioning she had undergone by Navy investigators and reporters and her eventual trip to Pensacola to join him.

When Jack had finished, Abe put his feet on his desk. "You are some sonnabitch! I don't think if I live to be a hundred I will ever hear another story like that." Then he started to shake with laughter and Jack soon joined him. As their mirth receded, Abe started asking questions about Jack's story. Jack responded fully -- except for not fully disclosing Chief Putty Benson's role in the deception.

"Well Jack, it looks like a voluntary confession addressed to your CO is the only route we can take. You've broken a lot of fuckin laws but as far as I can see you haven't done anyone any harm except for John Deal's relatives who apparently didn't care very deeply about that SOB. You haven't taken funds illegally, you haven't drawn any Navy funds for being a married man -- never cross the fuckin paymasters, and except for a few 'minor' cases of misrepresentation you haven't defrauded the government. What you have done is hold the Navy of this here United States up to ridicule. You've shown that they can't keep track of their officers. That they have awarded its highest decorations to the wrong man. That a skilled operator can hoodwink a series of commanding officers."

Putting his feet down from his desk and hunching his bulk over it, he looked Jack straight in the eyes and said, "What we've got to do is keep from rubbing salt in the wound unless forced to while at the same time confessing the deception. Then we throw you on the mercy of the court -- and there will be a court martial -- even with those 18 Jap planes you shot down and the two Navy Crosses that you won for John Deal -- one of which was awarded by Admiral Chester W. Nimitz hisself. But the first thing we got to do is hold off that fuckin Weymouth till tomorrow morning while you and I craft your confession."

Chapter 9 - Confession

From: Ensign Jack Dell, USNR

To: Commanding Officer, Naval Air Station, Pensacola

Subj: A voluntary statement concerning the identity of Lieutenant John Deal USNR

1. This statement is made voluntarily, with the advice of legal counsel, and with full knowledge that I may be subject to disciplinary action by cognizant naval authorities. I acknowledge that the statements made herein could be used against me in a trial by court martial.

2. In summary, between 12 June 1943 and 15 August 1944 I wrongfully assumed the identity of Ensign, Lieutenant junior grade, and Lieutenant John Deal USNR. By this statement I affirm that I am in fact Ensign Jack Dell and not Lieutenant John Deal. I undertook the deception so that I could see active service in the Pacific rather than be ordered back to the United States as the result of a trial by summary court martial. I am solely responsible for the deception and its consequences. I received no encouragement or assistance from anyone in the naval service in carrying out the deception. The purpose of this statement is to set the record straight and accept such action as the Navy sees fit to take. The statements herein are the full truth to the best of my knowledge.

3. The relevant facts are as follows and I stand ready to submit to questioning about these facts.

a. On 5 June 1943 while I was assigned to VF-321 at NAS Lahaina, TH, I was found guilty by a summary court martial of the charges of assault, destruction of private property, conduct prejudicial to good order and discipline, and conduct unbecoming an officer of the naval service. The sentence was loss of three months pay, restriction to quarters for one month, and a recommendation to the Chief of Naval Personnel that I revert to enlisted status. This sentence was approved by the convening authority on 12 June 1943 and I was ordered back to NAS Pensacola for further processing.

b. On the same day (12 June 1943) that I Ensign Jack Dell was to be detached, Ensign John Deal also attached to VF-321 at NAS Lahaina was killed in an aircraft operational accident at Kahoolawe target. At the time of his death Ensign Deal was in possession of orders (that resided in his personal effects) and a detaching endorsement by our Commanding Officer, detaching him for duty with VF-241 then in the South Pacific.

c. On the day of his death I was ordered by squadron authorities to inventory Ensign Deal's personal effects and as a matter of convenience deliver the various official messages associated with Deal's death to base communications. I conducted the inventory but retained Deal's orders and records. I failed to deliver the death messages to base communications. And I wrongfully disposed of his personal effects. At that point I decided to assume Deal's identity and carry out his orders.

d. I have no information as to whether personnel in VF-321 ever became aware of this deception, and if aware what actions they may have taken.

e. I, Ensign Jack Dell, reported as Ensign John

Deal to VF-241, then at Tavabatu in the Solomon Islands. I remained with the squadron until wounded in combat over Buin in the Solomons on 27 November 1943. During my tour in VF-241 as John Deal I was promoted to LTJG on 3 September 1943 and to Lieutenant on 1 November 1943. An extract of my operational record as John Deal while attached to VF-214 is at Tab A.

      f. From 30 November 1943 until 27 February 1944 I was assigned (as John Deal) to Naval Hospital, Oak Knoll, Calif. for treatment of wounds received in combat.

      g. Upon completion of rehabilitation at Oak Knoll I served (again as John Deal) in VF-277 embarked in USS President during combat operations in the Marshalls and the Mariannas. When detached from VF-277 on 1 August 1944 I was serving as the acting commanding officer of the squadron because the assigned commanding officer had been killed in an operational accident.

      h. On or about 15 August 1944 while en route to John Deal's next assignment with the Bureau of Naval Personnel in Washington, DC, I resumed my true identity as Jack Dell, but continued to wear the rank of Lieutenant earned as John Deal. I carried out my original June 1943 orders to NAS Pensacola after making erroneous entries in my personnel records. For reasons I don't understand there was never any record of my summary court martial in that record or in the orders I received to return to the United States in June 1943.

      i. I have served at NAS Pensacola from 15 September 1944 to the date of this statement. I am as of today wearing the insignia of my true rank, Ensign, USNR.

j. At no time while using the identity of Lieutenant John Deal did I accept any of his pay or allowances.

4. I am ready to cooperate fully with the Navy to correct the official records associated with Ensign John Deal USNR and Ensign Jack Dell USNR. All decorations received by me as John Deal are returned with this letter.

Very Respectfully,

/s/ Jack Dell

Tab A Operational record of Lieutenant John Deal (i.e., Ensign Jack Dell) while serving in VF-321, VF-241, and VF-277

Attachments: Navy Cross medals (2), Distinguished Flying Cross medals (4), Air Medals (8), Order of the Purple Heart Medal (1), Navy Commendation Medal (1), Pacific Theater Campaign Medal (4 battle stars).

Neither Jack nor Abe thought it necessary to bring Maggie into this letter of confession. Although Maggie did not consider herself now as an injured party, it remained to be seen how the State of California would view his falsification of the information on their marriage license. As Jack reviewed the letter he thought it was not much to show for two years of deception, heartache, and worry. He heaved a sigh of relief as he signed it.

As Abe reviewed the signed product of 24 hours of drafting and redrafting, he said, "This little baby will be a bombshell. The CO will shit in his britches when he reads it. No way can he avoid publicity and he won't get much help from his chain of command. No one will make admiral on the basis of acting on all this. The cards you hold are your combat record, your willingness to confess before exposed, and the threat of going to the newspapers with your case. But a lot of Navy blue red hots will want your ass. The next step is for me to run this by Commander Murphy -- strictly as a courtesy to my boss -- and then it goes to the skipper's office. Brace yourself. The next few weeks will be excitin' as hell. If I were you I would go to sleep with Momma one more time before you have visitors. Good luck, Jack. Oh, by the way, I hope you will ask for me as your defense counsel at your court martial. If I know Murphy, now that the family jewels are on the table he will want to get my black ass out of the limelight."

Late that evening Jack borrowed an old set of ensign's bars from Abe and pinned them on the collar of his uniform shirt. Early the next morning a shore patrol van picked him up and delivered him to the Bachelor Officers' Quarters. The two shore patrolmen were burly, tight lipped, and none too gentle. He was met at the BOQ by the air station personnel officer, Commander Ben Aldrich, who required Jack to sign his orders placing him on restriction. He was to remain in the BOQ and take all his meals there until further notice. He was not authorized to receive visitors except officers on official business. Nothing was said about phone calls.

The next day Jack was visited by Abe Smith. "These bastards are shitting bananas. The CO has ordered a pre-trial investigation but the only evidence available is your statement and your service record. They still think you may be a psychopath who is trying to con them. Some of them think you really killed Mr. John fucking Deal and that your confession is only a way to keep them away from your real crimes. Hell, Commander Murphy still thinks you are John Deal masquerading as Jack Dell. It is going to take a week for these shitheads to get their heads on straight. In the meantime they are sending messages all over the fucking world trying to verify your story."

"But the good news is I have a letter appointing me officially as your attorney. It wasn't easy because Murphy wanted to appoint some sonnofabitch he could control. I think he is scared of me, but he also thinks I am such a dumb black bastard that he can roll me if he has to."

A week later a pre-trial hearing chaired by the Administrative Officer was held in the Air Station legal office. The only question before the hearing officer was whether there was sufficient evidence to warrant preparing charges against Jack. Jack on Abe's advice waived his right to call witnesses and present evidence. On the tenth day of his restriction the charges were officially presented to Jack and he was required to acknowledge their receipt. Although set forth on official Navy forms and in stilted legalese their essential points were as follows:

That Ensign Jack Dell USNR between 12 June 1943 and 15 August 1944 did wrongfully and knowingly:

1. Impersonate another officer

2. Alter or dispose of official Navy records, correspondence, and communications without proper authority

3. Absent himself from his duty station

4. Make false official statement

5. Usurp authority

6. Accept promotions and awards not legally his to receive

7. Apply for and accept pay and allowances on behalf of another member of the service

8. Engage in conduct prejudicial to good order and discipline and unbecoming a commissioned officer Abe laughed when he read the charges to Jack, "This is as close to throwing the fuckin book at someone as I have seen. Well, we ain't going to contest any of these charges -- except maybe number seven. But we are going to have those high priced trial lawyers flown in from Washington think we will fight them all."

Two days later Jack was served papers that assigned the charges for trial by a General Court Martial to be held ten days hence in the Main Conference Room at Naval Air Station Pensacola. He was also served papers that stated his pre-trial restriction would continue because of his admitted past behavior as a fugitive.

That evening an article appeared on the second page of the Pensacola Journal stating that a naval officer assigned to the air station had impersonated another officer, had become a war hero while in that role, and was now facing a general court martial. In the days that followed, the story gained momentum and the wire services picked it up. Reporters started to show up at the BOQ attempting to gain interviews but were turned away by the masters-at-arms on duty. One confrontation turned into a scuffle and the reporter was arrested for trespass on government property. Though the reporter was quickly released, the Journal ran front page stories about the incident and then rehashed the story. But there was a new twist: accusations of Navy cover-up and a legal system run amok.

Both Jack and Abe were questioned under oath about leaking the story to reporters and swore they had not been in contact with the press. The strength of the guard at the BOQ was increased and instead of Jack's taking his meals in the BOQ dining room they were brought to his room. Jack was not permitted to make phone calls unless he submitted a special request to the Commanding Officer. The press complained that phone calls were headed off by the air station switch board. The tenor of news stories suggested a rapid souring of relations between local journalists and the administration of the naval air station.

On the day his court martial was to convene, Jack was picked up in the middle of the night by two officers in civilian clothes and taken to an anteroom off the courtroom where he was held under guard. It was a haggard, unshaven, weary, and hungry Jack Dell who was taken before the court at 0830 that morning.

Chapter 10 - Court Martial

As Jack was brought into the conference room he faced a long table covered with a green felt cloth. Behind the table were seven officers in Service dress blue uniforms. One Captain, four Commanders, and two Lieutenant Commanders. In front of and off to the sides of the long table were two smaller tables also covered with green felt cloths. Behind the one to the right were two officers in blues, Lieutenant Commanders who wore the star of the line but whose absence of any meaningful service ribbons told Jack they were the trial attorneys -- hired guns from Washington most likely since he had never laid eyes on them. At the table to the left was Lieutenant junior grade Abraham Lincoln Smith -- who gave Jack a wink.

Jack was still in the wash khaki uniform he had hurriedly dressed in the night before. At any rate he didn't have a blue uniform with an ensign's stripe on it. He was ushered to Abe's side by a master-at-arms. As he was about to sit in the chair designated by Abe, a booming voice from the captain at the long table ordered "All stand. The recorder will swear in the court."

The "recorder" seemed to be another word for the counsel presenting the government's case against one Ensign Jack Dell because one of the two lieutenant commanders at the adjacent table rose and swore in the court. The captain, apparently the "President" of the court, then swore in all the attorneys representing the government and the defendant. When all these oaths had been sworn, the Captain looked across the two tables at Jack.

Captain Anson "Anse' Hughes was the skipper of Naval Auxiliary Air Station, Saufley Field, near NAS Pensacola. He had been a dive bomber squadron skipper at Midway, a carrier air group commander during the landings at Guadalcanal, and executive officer of a carrier during the "Mariannas Turkey Shoot." He had the service ribbons to match. He was tall, spare man with a wispy thatch of prematurely gray hair. Worry lines -- too much combat? -- crossed his leathery face. His eyes were a light blue above a once too often broken nose and he had a way of fixing his stare on a person so that there was no doubt as to who was boss.

He asked Abe, "Why is the accused out of uniform and not very well turned out in what he is wearing?"

"Sir, if I may confer with my client for a moment I will answer that question."

A nod from Captain Hughes gave assent.

"Sir, my client was awakened at 0300 this morning at his place of restriction at the BOQ. He was not given time to shave and did not have the proper uniforms in his room to wear to this court. He has been kept waiting in an anteroom to this court room since 0330. He has not had breakfast, sir."

Captain Hughes turned to the recorder of the court and said, "Mr. Davenport, do you represent the commanding officer of the air station in these proceedings?"

Lieutenant Commander Hugh Davenport, JAG Corps, USN rose to his feet. "Yes sir, I am on loan from the Office of the Judge Advocate General in Washington to present the government's case. I am not responsible for the appearance of the accused, sir."

Davenport was a short, alert, handsome young man who looked even for wartime much too young to be wearing a lieutenant commander's stripes. He looked for the moment as though he had been distracted from more important business by the Court President's question.

"Mr. Davenport, I asked you a simple question. Do you represent the Commanding Officer of the Naval Air Station in these proceedings?"

Davenport looked around the room and then at Jack before answering. "Yes sir."

"Has the accused been convicted of any crime that you are aware of?"

"No, sir."

"Well Mr. Davenport, since the Commanding Officer of Naval Air Station Pensacola is not present and you are -- according to the charge sheet before the court-- presenting the Government's case at the direction of the commanding officer, you are responsible for the pre-trial treatment and appearance of the accused this morning. I hold you in contempt of this court for failing to provide for the well being of the accused as he is presented for trial. Specifically, I hold you responsible for harassment of the accused in violation of Navy regulations and for failing to see that he was properly fed and clothed before being presented before this court. Do you have anything to say on this matter."

These words hit Davenport like a thunderbolt.

While he knew Navy law, he had paid scant attention to Navy regulations and the customs of the service. Moreover, he had heard that many "old salts" (who in his opinion knew little of the law) never missed an opportunity to tweak members of a profession they held in contempt. These thoughts passed through his mind as stammered out,

"Sir, I will talk to the station CO and see that it doesn't happen again...."

"Hold it, Mr. Davenport. I said you were responsible. Being responsible means that you can't delegate or otherwise place your obligations on another officer's shoulders. Of course, you may talk to whomever you want, but you are an officer of this court and I demand that you follow Navy regulations to say nothing of the requirements of common decency. Do you understand, Mr. Davenport?"

Davenport was clearly not accustomed to being lectured on his duties in a court martial. He started to say something, thought better of it, and stopped in mid sentence before changing his response.

"Yes sir, I request a recess sir while we get the accused bathed, fed and in proper uniform."

"Granted. But if you make a practice of wasting this court's time, it will prejudice the government's case and I will report your conduct to the authority convening this court martial -- and to those who may be even more important to you, your superiors in Washington. The court will be in recess for two hours and reconvene at 1045."

Jack was taken out to an adjacent office to the undisguised glee of Abe Smith. "Wow, the old man really wire brushed that Yale Law smart ass. Really threw him off his feed. At least we are starting out with the moral upper hand. Never met a line officer yet who didn't want to shove it to a JAG motherfucker -- present company excepted. But I'm really enjoying this."

Two hours later Jack was back in court washed, fed, and in his blue service uniform snatched from Maggie's hands by a worried officer dispatched to their home. There followed a frantic bout with a pair of scissors as the Lieutenant's stripes were taken off the uniform leaving the single gold band of an ensign -- but with the star of the line adrift at an unseemly distance above the stripe. To Jack it was just another sign of chaos his world had become.

"Are you ready to proceed, Mr. Davenport?"

"Yes sir, and I apologize to the court and defense counsel for mistreatment of the accused." Receiving a nod from Captain Hughes he continued, "Sir, I would like to read the charges into the record." In the minutes that followed the charges were read and the defense was asked how the accused pleaded. Abe rose to his feet.

"Sir, the defendant pleads guilty to all charges except number seven concerning wrongful appropriation of pay and allowances -- to which he pleads not guilty. May I point out to the court that the defendant's voluntary confession that counsel for the government will place in evidence already admits to the other charges?"

"One thing at a time, Mr. Smith. We will get to Mr. Dell's statement in the government's own time. Will the defendant please rise."

"Mr. Dell, how do you plead to these charges?"

"Sir, I plead guilty to all charges except seven.

"Do you understand that in so doing you admitting to each and every element of the individual charges -- except for charge seven.

"Yes sir, I do."

"Do you realize that in so doing, you may not enter any defense to them?

"Yes sir, I do."

"Very well, the pleas are accepted and will be entered into the record. The government may proceed with its case on charge seven."

These pleas and their acceptance clearly disconcerted the Government's attorney because he had built his case on a set of interlocking pieces of evidence to encompass all the charges. His brief was a legal thing of beauty, but it was awkward in responding to the need of proving a single charge. He risked raising the ire of the court by going over material to which Jack had already entered a guilty plea. The upshot was that Davenport made a number of missteps in presenting evidence that apparently had nothing to do with the charge before the court. Murmurs from restless but unneeded witnesses in the hall distracted the court from the proceedings. Finally after a morning and early afternoon of attempting over frequent objections to prove that Jack had embezzled government funds, Davenport gave up and withdrew the charge.

Jack stood accused only of what he had already admitted to. Captain Hughes proceeded rapidly to close the court for findings on the remaining charges. Fifteen minutes later, Jack and Abe were called before the court and to no great surprise the guilty verdict was announced to a standing Jack Dell.

"The court is adjourned to 0830 tomorrow morning to hear matters in aggravation, extenuation, and mitigation. Mr. Davenport, I expect Mr. Dell to be treated decently and to be presentable tomorrow morning." As Jack left the court in the company of the masters-at-arms, he was accosted by two reporters and a photographer in the hallway. "What is the verdict? Have you been railroaded? Do you have anything to say? Jack remained silent and as quietly as possible was rushed out of the building to return to the BOQ.

That evening in Jack's room after supper, he and Abe went over their strategy. "The real action starts tomorrow, Jack. Davenport gets to present matters in aggravation to start the ball rolling. They will try to portray you as a vicious opportunist with a prior record of anti-social behavior. They may try to drag Maggie into this. If they do, I must ask her to testify. If we don't, you will come across as a monster and you are dead both in court and in the press. We've got one pissed off press. They are on your side and the Navy is starting to feel the heat -- persecuting one of its real genuine war heroes just because he tried to get in the war and do his duty. You know the rest. I don't know how they are getting this information but whoever it is really turning up the heat on whoever is going to review the record of this court martial. "After Davenport tries to do his worst, we get our turn at bat for extenuation -- what prompted you to act as you did -- and mitigation -- what a fucking hero you are. I want you to promise me that you won't get angry at Davenport and his questions. Don't lose your cool, particularly if I have to call Maggie! And, oh yeah, we have a few cards they -- and you -- don't know about yet. At this point it is better you don't know what they are. Now turn in and get some sleep, I want you to look your best in the morning -- alert, standing up straight, clear eyed -- a real hero who is being shit on!"

Over an ample breakfast the next morning, overseen by two solicitous stewards mates, Jack read the morning paper. There was a two column headline on the first page: "Navy Looking to Railroad War Hero." The details in the story made it apparent that the reporter had an informant in the courtroom or close to it. The reporter also managed to weave his story into a backdrop of the public's disgust with military justice. A sidebar to the story outlined John Deal's combat record and list of decorations. Jack threw the paper down in disgust and finished his coffee.

When the court reconvened, Captain Hughes shot a question at Jack: "Mr. Dell, do you believe you have received a fair trial to this point?"

"Yes sir."

"Have you been in contact with anyone other than counsel about this case since you were charged?

"No sir."

"Do you have any knowledge about how this case has gained the publicity it has?

"No sir."

"Very well, Mr. Davenport, you may proceed to introduce matters in aggravation."

Lieutenant Commander Davenport rose and said, "Mr. President, I would like to remind the court respectfully that Mr. Dell's statement already introduced in evidence states that he was convicted by a special court martial in June 1943 for destruction of property, assault, and conduct unbecoming an officer. This officer clearly has a past record of violent and unlawful behavior. Indeed, his conviction served as the trigger to his path of deceit over the past two years. I would ask the court to consider this prior conviction in adjudging sentence in this case."

The President turned to Abe, "Mr. Smith do you have anything to say in response?"

"Yes sir, there is no evidence before this court of a prior court martial conviction of Ensign Dell. The government has gone to great trouble to make the case that he is a liar and a deceitful person. Yet now it is relying on the defendant's own statement to make a case for aggravation. I believe that the government has an obligation to produce the court martial record and the action of the reviewing authority on that record before accepting Mr. Dell's statement as to his prior conviction."

"Well, Mr. Davenport?"

"Sir, I would like to call Mr. Schuyler Spencer of the Bureau of Naval Personnel's records division -- Pers R -- to address that question."

Mr. Spencer was a bespeckled man who was badly near-sighted. His heavy lenses and the frown lines on his forehead suggested a mole who had suddenly been exposed to daylight and found the experience distasteful. He was sworn and with Jack's Navy Department personnel record before him was quizzed about a prior conviction. Spencer thumbed back and forth through the pages of Jack Dell's service record but found no court martial documents.

Abe questioned Benson. "Mr. Spencer, has Mr. Dell ever had access to his record kept in your office?

"No sir, I am the official custodian of his record and thousands of others. While an officer may have access to his official record if he comes to Washington, there is no record in our log of Mr. Dell's ever exercising that privilege."

"So, while Mr. Dell has been convicted of altering the copy of the service record in his possession, there is no way he could alter his official record kept in the Bureau of Naval Personnel. Is that correct?"

"Yes sir, You need to understand that there are two copies of any officer's record. The first is the official record retained in the Bureau of Naval Personnel. It is complete and it provides the basis for assignments, promotions, discharges and other personnel actions. The second record is only a partial extract of the official record -- mostly carbon copies -- and is kept by the officer's command except when the officer is in transit, in which case it is sent -- usually but not always sealed -- to the officer's new command in the officer's own albeit temporary custody."

"Is it correct to say that if there is no record of

court martial in an officer's record held by the Bureau of Naval Personnel, that officer was never convicted by court martial?"

Spencer squirmed under this question before answering, "It would not signify that he had never been convicted by a court martial, only that the record of that court martial -- if there were one -- had never been forwarded to the Bureau of Naval Personnel. I know of no case where the system has made such an error."

Abe turned to face the President of the Court and said in a low voice, "Sir, unless the government can show an official record of conviction by court martial, I request that the attempt to use Mr. Dell's statement about such conviction be denied by the court."

Captain Hughes turned to look at Jack. "Mr. Dell you cannot be forced to testify, but do you want to say anything about the court martial you cited in your statement."

"No sir, I am satisfied with my statement."

"Very well, the Court rules that Ensign Dell's voluntary statement can be used against him as evidence in the absence of government documentation substantiating a court martial conviction."

Abe rose to his feet. "Sir, I object. Even though Mr. Dell admitted to a court martial conviction, the government has presented no evidence of the convening or reviewing authorities action on his conviction -- if any. I discussed this matter with the Staff Judge Advocate of Commander Air Forces Pacific Fleet day before yesterday, and he stated to me, after consulting command records, that the conviction of Ensign Dell was thrown out by the reviewing authority because of fatal flaws of procedure in the pre-trial investigation and in the conduct of the trial itself. His words were: 'It was a botched job done in a hurry. 'Counsel can check with the Air Pac staff to verify this point."

Captain Hughes got very red in the face and snarled at Abe, "Mr. Smith, do you mean to tell me you have been sitting on this evidence while we have spent valuable time trying to establish whether or not Mr. Dell had been convicted? It looks to me like you have been sandbagging the government and this court."

"Sir, I have no documents to support my point. Moreover, I did not believe the government would introduce a prior conviction as a matter of aggravation without evidence other than Mr. Dell's confession to make the point. I would rather the subject had not come up, or when it did that you would have ruled against the government in the absence of documentation. I apologize for any embarrassment caused the court, but I respectfully submit that it is for the government to make its own case, not rely on Mr. Dell's statement for support when their effort to this point has been to paint him as a deceiver and a liar."

"Very well. The court rescinds its earlier judgment and will not accept Mr. Dell's statement as evidence of a court martial conviction until such time as the government can prove that Mr. Dell's conviction was approved by the convening authority and the reviewing authority. Mr. Davenport, do you wish to pursue the court martial conviction further? Verify it yourself with COMAIRPAC's legal officer?"

"If it please the court, I would like to confer with my colleague." An animated conversation of several minutes followed between the two government trial attorneys. Finally, Davenport rose and faced the court.

"No sir, the government withdraws its evidence of a prior court martial conviction and has no additional matters to present in aggravation."

"Since the government has no more evidence or witnesses to call, the court will move on to matters of extenuation. Mr. Smith, you may present your case."

Abe rose to his feet after putting his notes aside on the table. "Mr. President and members of the court, I would ask that you place yourself in the shoes of Mr. Dell in mid July 1943. He was twenty years old. An ensign in the Navy, right out of flight training. He had gotten into a scrape and was court martialed. He was desperately eager to get into the war. Note that by his admitted deception he chose to go into combat in a stinking hole in the Solomons instead of coming back to the sunny beaches of Pensacola. He made mistakes, but he also made a choice. He didn't know that his court martial conviction would be overturned a month later. He was faced with disgrace or a chance to serve his country.

"Mr. Dell could easily have been killed in the Solomons. Many of his sqadron-mates were. If Mr. Dell had been killed serving his country in the air over the Solomons, we wouldn't be trying him here today. Instead we would be mourning him and others like him for the sacrifices made. I dare say each member of this court has lost a close shipmate or buddy in the war that ended two months ago. (a pause here while Abe looked at each member of the court in turn) Some of those shipmates or buddies weren't perfect in life, but we mourn them anyway. Mr. Dell wasn't perfect either, but he survived and they didn't. So we are in a situation where the dead are allowed their well-deserved peace, but the living are left to face a jury of their peers. Mr. Dell has admitted his transgressions, the dead didn't live long enough to face disciplinary action for theirs.

"I ask each member of the court: Have you never made a mistake? Have you never broken Navy Regulations? Have you never been sorry that you did the wrong thing? What course would you have taken if you had been in Mr. Dell's shoes and were to be sent home rather than to fight for your country? Was his choice so reprehensible? Would you have wanted Mr. Dell flying on your wing? If a Jap were on your tail, would you have wanted Mr. John Deal -- rest his immortal soul -- or Mr. Jack Dell dealing with him to see that you lived to fight another day? Is it too far fetched to say that some naval aviators are living today because Jack Dell and not John Deal did fly on their wing? Later in these proceedings I will discuss Mr. Dell's combat record while carrying the name of Mr. John Deal. What I ask of you now is think of the man who took the hard path, a path he probably often regretted taking after a tough day in the slime and filth and disease of the Solomons and experiencing the loss of a friend in the air. He did not take the easy way -- and you, we, are now judging him because he took the law and regulations into his own hands. He didn't do it the Navy way, but by everything that is holy, he did it in a way that John Paul Jones -- no saint either I might add -- would understand: 'I will fight the enemy, I will not give up, I will not let the peacetime rules and the lawyers keep me from the fight. And fight I will. And when it is over, as it must be, I will face a jury of my peers and tell them: I did what was right!'

"The great Nelson said: 'No commander can do wrong by laying his ship alongside one of the enemy. 'Gentlemen of the court, Mr. Dell laid his ship alongside those of the enemy, and I submit to you, that in so doing he did no wrong that a fighting Navy cannot understand and forgive!"

The court sat in stunned silence at this speech -- and the eloquent rolling cadences of its delivery. It was an appeal to the gut, not the head. The members of the court stared at the green cloth on the table in front of them for a few moments before Captain Hughes raised his head and said, "Mr. Davenport, what is your response to Mr. Smith's eloquent words about Mr. Dell's conduct and our Navy's history?"

"Mr. President, our country is a nation of laws -- and Mr. Dell broke some of them. The emotion of battle does not change that. We have many heroes who did not break the law. While Mr. Smith makes the emotional case, the fact of the matter is more likely that Mr. Dell made his choice not out of a desire to serve his country but out of a desire to escape punishment, to evade his results of his escapades. I am not an historian, but I suspect that while Nelson and John Paul Jones bent the rules, they were not liars and law breakers."

The President considered this response for a moment, and then said, "I am not so sure of that, Mr. Davenport. You must have heard of Nelson's 'blind eye' at the Battle of Copenhagen, an offense that could have resulted in a court martial and a sentence of being shot on his own flagship's quarter-deck. John Paul Jones may have been the biggest maverick in our Navy's history. But we are not here for a history lesson. Mr. Smith makes a case based on a fighting Navy that doesn't always do things by the book and you make a case based on the law. And in making that distinction the law always wins until they can be changed to fit the needs of a fighting organization. In any event the court will take both your and Mr. Smith's remarks into consideration as it considers matter of extenuation."

Abe again rose to his feet and sought the attention of the President of the Court. "Sir, I cannot let stand without challenge the Government's charge that Ensign Jack Dell is a liar and a cheat. To whom did he lie or cheat? The American people? I don't think so. His commanding officers?

They are both dead, but if the Court pleases, I can introduce evidence from Navy records that refutes such a charge. Did he lie or cheat with his squadron mates during the war? Hell no! He saved the lives of some of them and put himself in great danger in the doing. I submit that the only party that was lied to, or cheated if you prefer, was the body of rules and regulations of the United States Navy and those more interested in the letter than the spirit of those rules and regulations. I ask the Court: Are you going to rule in favor of the lawyers or the fighters? Whose side are you on...."

"That will do, Mr. Smith. I will not have you impugning the motives or judgment of the court or its officers. You have made your point -- eloquently and with passion -- but you put aside too quickly the concept of duty, the duty of Mr. Dell and the duty of this court. "If neither counsel has any other matters of extenuation to present we will turn to matters of mitigation. Mr. Smith you may present your case."

Abe again rose. But this time he pulled a small package from his pocket. He emptied its contents on the table in front of him. A collection of service ribbons tumbled out onto the felt cloth. He looked at them for a moment and then looked up at the court.

"Gentlemen, you have all seen the medals these bright ribbons represent. Some of you wear similar ribbons on your blue service uniform. You won them the hard way. No one gave them to you. You had to bet your life on more than one occasion. And a grateful country pinned a medal on your chest. I don't wear any of these awards -- nor does counsel for the government. But you can bet we would be proud to deserve wearing them.

"Mr. Dell is an unusual naval officer. The government has painted him as deceitful, a liar, a lawbreaker, self-serving, and other words you have heard in this court over the last two days. I would portray him a little differently. Here is an officer who twice won our Navy's second highest combat award -- the Navy Cross. The Navy doesn't pass them out like candy -- as some would say is the case with awards presented to staff officers somewhat farther from the sound of guns. Here is an officer who won almost every medal a combat airman can win. And he gained them when the going was the toughest. Midway and Coral Sea I am told were tougher, but few would say that slogging through the Solomons on the ground, on the sea, or in the air was any picnic.

"Mr. Dell is a warrior. He is not a peacetime sailor. But it is peacetime justice bringing a warrior before the bar. Mr. Dell broke the Navy's law. But, oh yes, he shot down the enemy in droves! We needed him over the Solomons and in the Mariannas. But his day is over, thank you very much. We don't need his kind any more. He now needs to pay up -- not for his victories over the enemy, but for his perhaps too intense desire to close and defeat the enemy. Mr. Dell, I am going to ask you to stand up and face the court.

Jack rose and with the respectful but unintimidated gaze perfected under Gus Prather's tutelage, he faced the members of the court and looked each one in the eye.

"Members of the court, you see standing before you, Ensign Jack Dell. You will notice that he wears no combat ribbons on his blue service uniform. There is no Navy Cross, no Distinguished Flying Cross, no Purple Heart, no battle stars on his chest. He is as bare as the newest nugget who just got his wings. Look at the insignia on his sleeves. He is not a lieutenant. No, he serves in the most junior officer grade in the Navy. To look at him you would not know that under that plain unadorned uniform lies a fighter, a winner of the Navy Cross -- not once, but twice just to prove it was no accident. You wouldn't know that at 22 years old he was probably the youngest acting skipper of a fighter squadron in our Navy's history. He was a skipper in combat, gentlemen. There is only one other person in this room who has skippered a squadron in combat, and he is in charge of these proceedings."

Looking at Jack, he said, "Mr. Dell, would you please raise the cuff on your right trouser leg to your knee?"

With some reluctance Jack did as he was asked, and the livid scar shown bright red and the missing flesh in his calf was obvious.

"Gentlemen of the court, Mr. Dell has already paid the price of his foolishness in disregarding the law. A Japanese anti-aircraft gunner over Buin marked paid to Mr. Dell's debt to the law. There are few in this room who have paid such a price. Mr. Dell fought the enemy, Gentlemen, and it wasn't all medals and victory parades -- you may sit down Mr. Dell. In conclusion, I ask the court to look at the man beneath the ensign's uniform. Ask yourself, what he owes his country and his Navy and what his country and his Navy owe him. How does it balance? He is not asking exoneration. He is not asking that the slate be wiped clean. He is asking for understanding. He is asking for compassion for a fighter who is back from the war, a fighter who gave all there was to give, a fighter who came close to having to give his life, a fighter who now that there is peace, and there is time to straighten out the record, faces disgrace. He was no disgrace over the Solomons and the Mariannas. Why should he be a disgrace in Pensacola?"

Captain Hughes, by now ready for Abe Smith's oratory, said, "Thank you, Mr. Smith, for your eloquent testimonial to American fighting men. Mr. Davenport, do you have any evidence to counter Mr. Smith's pleas?"

Davenport got slowly to his feet, "Sir, an officer has come forward and would offer evidence that Mr. Dell's combat record is not all that it has been represented to be. I would like to call Lieutenant Commander Jethro Stuart to testify."

Jeb Stuart entered the room in well fitting blues and the brand new stripes of a Lieutenant Commander. He had put on weight, but still walked with his self confident gait. He looked at Jack with a slight frown, took the witness chair and was sworn in.

Lieutenant Commander Davenport asked, "Would you identify yourself and your duty station, please?"

"Lieutenant Commander Jethro Stuart, United States Navy. I am assigned to the staff of Naval Air Advanced Training in Corpus Christi, Texas."

'Where and when did you know Ensign Jack Dell?"

"First of all, when I knew him he was Lieutenant John Deal. We were both assigned to VF-277 in the President from late winter to mid summer of 1944."

"What were your assignments in VF-277?"

"Initially, I was assigned as XO of the squadron and Deal -- or Dell -- was one of the pilots without any significant ground duties. Later because a SNAFU in seniorities and because our skipper was killed, Deal -- or Dell -- was made CO while I remained as XO."

"So you worked for a while as Mr. Dell's superior and then as his subordinate. Is that correct?"

"Yes sir."

"How was that relationship? Use your own words to describe Mr. Dell's performance and demeanor."

"Deal came to the squadron as a hot shot ace from the Solomons where he had been shot up. He collected a bunch of medals, including a Navy Cross. He was a loner and didn't fit in well in the squadron. While I was XO we got along, but we weren't buddies either. I always felt he swaggered a bit and got more mileage than he needed out of his combat record."

"Tell the court the circumstances as to how he leapfrogged you to become acting CO on your skipper's death."

"Well, Deal -- or Dell -- didn't want to be XO even though he was a few numbers senior to me. So he conned the CO into letting him bow out of the XO job. As next most senior I moved into the XO slot. It was sort of crazy but that's the way things were. You put the best man where he was most needed. Well, I mean......Dell didn't seem to want responsibility and I was willing to do the job. After the skipper was killed, I assumed I would be made CO but CAG saw it differently and jumped Deal in over me. Deal and CAG always seemed to hit it off. I think he was awed by Deal's combat record. He and the other COs were always asking him for advice."

"Mr. Stuart, what kind of an aviator was Mr. Dell or Deal?"

"He was a hot shot. He always seemed to be where there was some glory and some Jap planes to be shot down. By June of '44 we were facing the Jap second team and he notched a big score during the 'Turkey Shoot. "I remember one time during the shoot when he took his division and ran off after some Jap 'leakers' leaving me to deal with the Jap escorting zeros. We had a confrontation about it, but the skipper sided with Deal and that was that."

"Mr. Stuart, Mr. Dell has been convicted of a number of offenses. His counsel has portrayed him as a fighter and a hero, an officer who should be forgiven for breaking the law because of the needs of combat. What is your reaction to this portrayal of Mr. Dell?"

"He was good at shooting down Japs, but I thought he was a lousy officer. An opportunist and a liar. I thought he had something to hide and that his retiring, leave-me-alone demeanor was an act. Underneath that exterior, I thought he was a tough, conniving son of a bitch!" Jeb Stuart looked at Jack as he said these last words with an expression that said "Up yours, Deal!"

Abe was on his feet with these last words, booming out, "I object, Mr. President. The witness is slandering Mr. Dell. Clearly, Mr. Stuart harbors a deep resentment against Mr. Dell. Moreover, their former skipper is dead and unable to speak to these insults."

"Objection overruled, Mr. Smith. Counsel was within his rights to ask Mr. Stuart his opinion of Mr. Dell.

Your witness, Mr. Smith."

Abe rose and started pacing in back of the defense's table. After a while he looked up and said, "Mr. Stuart, how long were you in combat?"

"Let's see. I would guess around five months in 1944 before I was ordered back to the staff in Corpus Christi."

"How many Japanese planes did you shoot down?"

At this Lieutenant Commander Davenport raised his hand and said, "Objection. Witness's combat record is not at issue here. The court is asked to have the defense withdraw the question."

"Objection overruled. The defense is given wide latitude in examining the motives of individuals who question the integrity of the defendant. Proceed, Mr. Smith."

"How many Japanese planes did you shoot down?"

"Two. And two probables."

"It was a long time ago but can you tell the court the approximate dates and circumstances of each instance, including the type of aircraft involved?"

"The first time was in the Spring of 1944 when the President's task group struck the Marshalls. I bagged a Japanese plane during the first day's raid."

"What kind of plane was it and where was he flying?"

"It was a Japanese scout seaplane that had just taken off to escape the strike. The Jap rear gunner was shooting back at me before I shot him down."

This dialogue had the court's rapt attention. Each

member was a pilot and most had been in combat and could weigh the difficulty or ease of the action described. Abe continued,

"And your second kill, Mr. Stuart?

"It was during the first day of the big shoot over the Mariannas. My division and Deal's division had high CAP to pick off the Jap fighters. After our initial engagement, the Japs broke up and most started for home. I took my division in pursuit. Deal got permission from the fighter director to go after some Kate leakers. He just went off haring after the easy stuff while we went after the Zekes. I bagged one Zeke during the long tail chase."

"Are you saying that you pursued retreating Jap fighters while Mr. Dell here broke off and went after Jap torpedo bombers that were inbound on the task force?"

"That's an unfair question. Our mission was to go after Jap fighters, not go after the easy pickings. Others had that job."

"But, Mr. Stuart -- and forgive me I have never been in combat -- doesn't the situation often change in combat? Sometimes, doesn't even the mission change to fit new developments. From what I hear air combat is a pretty confusing place and there are no cookie cutter solutions to tactical problems."

Again Davenport rose, "Objection. Counsel is impugning witness's judgment, a judgment that is irrelevant to the matter at hand."

Abe turned from Stuart to address the President of the Court." Sir, I am trying to establish that the witness harbored ill will against Mr. Dell, an ill will founded on jealousy of his combat record and his own lack of combat experience."

"Very well, Mr. Smith, proceed, but try to keep to the point. We are not refighting the Mariannas Turkey Shoot here, we are examining matters in mitigation as they apply to Mr. Dell."

"Thank you, Mr. President. Mr. Stuart, why did you feel it necessary to appear as a witness at Mr. Dell's court martial? Did you seek out the government or did it seek you out?

"I came forward, Mr. Smith, to do my duty. I always felt that Deal skated along and was not surprised that he was accused of deceit, false statements, and the rest of it. It was time he paid the price."

"Do you feel any regret in appearing in a trial of a former shipmate, your former commanding officer, and inferring that he did his duty only to serve himself?"

"I feel that I had to come forward and state the facts -- and when asked, my opinions."

"If you were to be judged by your shipmates and superiors, would you expect the same candor and ruthless pursuit of the truth?"

Jeb Stuart answered with a smirk, "Yes, I would."

Abe turned to pick up some notes on his desk. Mr. President, while we still have Mr. Stuart on the stand, I would like to introduce in evidence a copy of a fitness report in Mr. John Deal's promotion jacket in the Bureau of Naval Personnel. This report covers the period of June through August 1944 while LT Deal was the acting CO of VF-277 and Mr. Stuart here was the XO."

As Captain Hughes nodded his assent, Abe started to read,

"This report to be submitted in evidence was filled out by Lieutenant Commander Jackson McDowell, then CAG 27. It says in part:

Lieutenant Deal is an outstanding combat aviator, one in a million. During the Battle of the Philippines Sea he demonstrated not just heroism but consummate combat skill by seeking a change of mission for his flight while airborne as the circumstances of combat changed. Assigned CAP to deal with Japanese fighters, he requested from the fighter director a change of mission for his division to go after penetrating Japanese torpedo bombers then threatening the task force. Other airborne flight leaders were not as perceptive of the changed situation and the new threat to the force. Deal's flexibility and combat awareness, prevented a major attack on the force by a determined enemy. During a single flight his division was credited with twelve kills of which eight were his....

"The report continues as follows...

When the commanding officer of his squadron was killed in an operational accident, I designated Dell as acting Commanding Officer over the executive officer of the squadron who had not shown as good judgment in combat and in leading the men of the squadron.

Abe looked up at Jeb Stuart and said,

"Was CAG McDowell describing you when he referred to 'other flight leaders were not as perceptive' and later as the executive officer "who had not shown as good judgment in combat and leading the men in the squadron?"

"I don't know who CAG was referring to."

"Perhaps we should recall Mr. Schuyler Spencer from BuPers to the witness chair and ask him to produce CAG's fitness report on you, since you relieved Mr. Deal -- or Dell -- as CO when he was ordered back to Pearl Harbor."

At this point, Captain Hughes had heard enough and said, "That will do Mr. Smith. Mr. Stuart you are excused. Mr. Smith, do you have anything else to add in mitigation? "

"Yes sir, I have before me a certified copy of a CINCPAC Fleet staff memorandum dated 15 August 1944. It is addressed to Admiral Nimitz. I would like to present it as evidence."

As Hughes nodded, Abe started to read,

From Staff Personnel Officer. To: Commander in Chief. Subject: Congressional Medal of Honor Nomination. Pursuant to your request to inquire into the eligibility of Lieutenant John Deal for the award of the Medal of Honor, nominations for this award can be initiated by any flag officer. However, the ultimate recommendation to the Secretary of the Navy is made by the Chief of Naval Operations. Lieutenant Deal's heroic performance on 18 June indicates he meets the eligibility requirements and we can prepare the necessary nomination if you desire. You will recall that you previously awarded him a Navy Cross (his second) last week for the same heroic action. The Admiral's attention is very respectfully invited to the fact that in view of the many Congressional Medal of Honor award nominations being sent forward, the criteria for the award are being made more stringent.

"There is a note on the margin that states: 'Send it forward. CWN' The notation 'Send it forward' is underlined."

"In a telephone call to the awards division of the Bureau of Naval Personnel I have been told that forwarding of the award nomination is being held in abeyance because no one can find Lieutenant John Deal. I would submit we have before us the officer whose exploits Admiral Nimitz thought sufficient to warrant award of the Medal of Honor. The Defense has nothing more to add in mitigation."

It was several moments before Captain Hughes after looking at Lieutenant Commander Davenport and Abe said, "The courtroom will be cleared while the court considers a sentence."

As they filed out, Jack was taken to an anteroom to await the sentence. It took longer than they thought it would and it was late afternoon before they were recalled.

Captain Hughes, looked at Jack and said. "Ensign Dell rise. The sentence of this court is that you are to be dismissed from the service, forfeit all pay and allowances, and to serve six months confinement in a naval prison to be selected by the Chief of Naval Personnel. The court recommends to the convening authority that he exercise leniency as he considers this sentence in view of your combat record and service. Let me add, Mr. Dell, that this court found its task most difficult. We are naval officers, not lawyers. But we are charged to follow the laws of the

Navy, not our sense of justice for officers who have seen as much combat as you have."

Jack looked at Captain Hughes as Gus Prather would have expected him to act. His head was high, and he looked directly at the President of the Court with respect and nodded his head.

"Do you have anything further to say, Mr. Dell?"

"No sir, I want to thank the court for a fair hearing.

"Very well, this court stands adjourned until such time as other cases are brought before it."

Chapter 11 - Justice

That evening thanks to the intercession of Captain Hughes with the air station commanding officer, Maggie was allowed to visit Jack. It was a tearful session. But, they agreed that as bad as the sentence was, at least they could rebuild their lives when Jack's prison time was over. They had managed to sufficiently comfort one another as to be able to welcome Abe when he came by later in the evening.

Abe reviewed the day. "Jack, those guys were just doing their jobs. The Navy way is let the court martial do the hatchet job and then let the CO be the good guy after they reach a verdict and set a sentence. The only bad news is that Murphy will be at the CO's side when he decides and I think he now has enough egg on his face that he is in no mood to recommend leniency. The other bad news is that the skipper is a hard-ass who came to aviation late -- somebody they call a 'johnny come lately' -- and he thinks like a battleship sailor. He has never been in combat in his life. He spent the whole war here in the training command." Abe snorted, "They say he was doing too important a job here to send him out to the war!"

"The good news is that these bastards are under a lot of pressure. The wire services have spread this court martial and the verdict all over the country. The reserves see this as the revenge of the regulars. The aviators see this as evidence of a battleship mindset. The old retireds see the whole episode as evidence of a general looseness in the Navy. The bleeding hearts see this as white Navy brass hats putting your uppity Jig lawyer in his place. And so on. Everyone seems to have an axe to grind. But John Q Public is upset that a personnel system he doesn't understand has somehow managed to crucify the boy next door who turns out to have been recommended for the Congressional Medal of Honor by none other than Admiral Chester W. Nimitz. One thing for sure, the CO's phone will be ringing off the hook with advice. I already see signs that the Navy's hierarchy is headed for cover. No glory in this dustup. No suh!"

"Where do we go from here, Abe? Just go quietly and serve my sentence?"

"No way! We continue to fight. After the CO acts to affirm or reduce the sentence, it goes to the Admiral for review. He is new. I don't have a read on him, but he can't be happy to have this tossed in his lap within weeks after reporting aboard. I hear the reporters are already camped outside his office and that he can't talk to any audience before the subject comes up. You got to understand what has the Navy riled is the pressure that they will be forced to set an unwanted precedent in letting a low level puke like you thumb his nose at the system. It seems like all the Bureau of Naval Personnel worries about is precedents, precedents that will endanger their precious policies. Exceptions to the rules just drive them bananas. They say they have to be fair to others, but what they really mean is that they like a steady course where they don't have to put their necks out very much."

" After the CO and the Admiral act then we have the whole appeal process. And it is lengthy. It could go on for a year or before we exhaust all remedies. But I should warn you when the CO affirms your conviction and sentence, he can pack you off to the station brig. He'll probably do just that but my guess is that the Admiral won't let him ship you off to Portsmouth until he gets his shot at the court record as reviewing authority.

"I don't know who is leaking the details of this story to the papers, but they are doing a good job of keeping the United States Navy on the hot seat. We just have to hope that some congressmen start to get interested and begin to put heat on the Secretary of the Navy to step in and straighten this all out."

As Abe predicted the skipper approved the verdict and the sentence as adjudged and Jack was picked up at the BOQ by the Marines in charge of the station brig. He was not treated gently. His head was roughly shaved, he was issued brig clothing, though he was confined in a cell separate from the general brig population. Each meal was made a production with two marines entering the cell one carrying a tray and the other a truncheon. The tray was slammed on the floor, and he was required to shout, "Thank you, SIR."

Once when he was slow with the required response, he was slammed across the legs with a truncheon and kicked. "Fuckin airdales" and similar epithets accompanied each contact with the guard force

Jack was taken out once a day in the exercise yard and run through a push up and sit up drill until he was exhausted. When returned to his cell, he was pushed roughly through the door and sent sprawling on the deck.

Contrary to every nerve in his body, he didn't fight back but picked himself up and vowed self control. He came to consider the guards as the Japanese enemy and he came to terms with his new environment.

A week after his incarceration, he received a visit from Abe. Abe was ushered into his cell to a hardly concealed "Your Jig-a-boo lawyer is here to see you." Abe said the Admiral would act on the case within a week and then he would be off to Portsmouth Prison or perhaps serve a reduced sentence in the brig. That night the guards, apparently thinking he wouldn't have any more visitors for a while, took turns working Jack over. He was left on the floor sobbing and spitting out blood. The next morning he still lay where he fell, his chest heaving as he cried out from the pain in his ribs and mouth. His breakfast and lunch were untouched, lying where they had been shoved through the door. In mid afternoon the officer-in-charge of the brig made his daily inspection and found Jack in delirium.

When Jack woke up he found himself in sickbay with a Marine guard at the door. A day later the Admiral sent for him, but he was told Jack was in no condition to be moved since he had "met with an accident in the station brig."

Rear Admiral Vernon Harding had a major problem. The commanding officer of an air station under his command had court martialed an officer of that command for impersonating another officer for a year during the war --among many other charges. An extraordinary case but one fully within the capabilities of the Navy's legal system. But there was a hooker: the impersonator was not only was a hero with two Navy Crosses, he had become a martyr to an excitable public as well. It was a martyrdom the press, and now the Congress, were happy to exploit as the military legal systems came under systematic attack from many quarters. Returning veteran's found sympathetic ears for listening to their wartime grievances.

Harding was a tall, thin, graying officer who had commanded a carrier, a sister ship of the President, in the Pacific, received his two stars, and was being groomed to be put out to pasture next year since the Navy now had too many admirals.

The case before him had built up into a political and public relations firestorm. A young man who had been nominated for the Medal of Honor had been convicted by a court martial and sentenced to dismissal from the service and imprisonment for six months. That asshole Cushing, the skipper of the air station, had bullheadedly affirmed the findings and the sentence instead of reducing them and getting the story off the front pages. But aside from the practical considerations, there was the moral issue (it said something about the Admiral's priorities that the moral issues came second) concerning the justice of harshly sentencing an officer with such a distinguished record. Less than half a dozen Navy pilots in the entire Pacific war had been nominated for the Congressional Medal of Honor and the old guard in their blind stupidity insisted on tracking one down and cutting his throat.

As he reviewed the record of the court martial together with Cushing's action as the convening authority, he came back to considering his decision. Never one to shrink from a difficult decision he considered his options. His own legal officer, a full captain in the judge advocate general corps, stood before him. He had prepared an endorsement that approved Cushing's action. Harding remembered the phone call he had received just that morning from the executive assistant to the Secretary of the Navy and another from the Vice Chief of Naval Operations asking what action he would take on the Dell case. "It's your decision, but you need to know that there is a lot of high level interest here -- and it is growing..."

Nervous nellies. They all wanted him to carry Cushing's can, but all were ready with catcalls from the sidelines if the hue and cry resulted in a reversal. Well, he could carry the can, but this case really bothered him....

Harding looked up from his desk at his judge advocate, Captain Ludlow Browning.

"Lud, I want to talk to this boy before I send him to Portsmouth. Get him up here."

"But, Admiral, you can't put yourself...

Harding cut him short with a wave of a hand. "Lud you mean well, but you need to understand that I am the Admiral and you are my legal officer. Get him up here, NOW!

Thirty minutes later Harding's chief of staff came in the room. Maxwell "Max" Steiner was an old friend and Academy classmate of Harding. He could and did speak frankly. "Vern, we can't get that boy up here right now. It seems he was taken from the brig to sick bay yesterday. Somehow he got injured, pretty badly, in the brig."

Harding threw down his eyeglasses and said "Goddam, what is that shithead Cushing up to? You don't have to tell me what has gone on in that brig. This breaks the fuckin limit. Get that fathead up here cause I'm going to work him over. While you are at it get whoever was the President of the court up here -- Anse Hughes wasn't it? We are going to sort out this fucked up mess."

An hour later the four captains, Max Steiner, Anse Hughes, Lud Browning, and Felix Cushing were standing before the Admiral. The Admiral looked over the group and then focused on each one and their role in this problem before saying, "I'll start with you Anse."

"I can't bring any pressure to bear on you Anse. You did your duty as you saw it in convicting and sentencing this boy. I want you to tell me as a naval officer -- not a fuckin ambulance chaser (pardon me, Lud) -- whether we, the Navy, did the right thing."

"Admiral, the boy admitted to the charges. The whole trial was about aggravation, extenuation, and mitigation. We had no choice but to find him guilty, unless we are ready to throw the whole court martial system out the window. I did my duty and there wasn't a knat's ass worth of room for discretion by the court except in the sentencing. Given the findings if we had sentenced him to any less, you could have had me up here for dereliction of duty. I pushed for the sentence that I did so that Felix would have some room to alter it to a lesser punishment. The real battle in this mess is not in the court but in the actions of the convening and reviewing authorities."

"Having said that I must say that Felix's people treated young Dell shabbily. He was brought before the court without a full night's sleep, unfed, in a slovenly uniform, and with a defense counsel right out of law school. Though I must say that sonavabitch did one of the best jobs I have ever seen in running rings around the JAG time servers (excuse me, Lud) I have seen. But it didn't end there. I had to go to Felix personally to let that boy see his wife after the sentencing. And I have heard that after Felix signed off on the record, Dell was hustled off to the tender mercies of the air station brig. If this guy really won two Navy Crosses, we have a lot on our consciences. Sorry Felix, I had to tell it like it is."

Harding turned to the skipper of the air station. "Felix, your story better be good because I 'm so pissed off, I may order an investigation as to how your air station's legal and confinement systems are being run."

Felix Cushing was not in the least intimidated by his admiral. He was a short, squat man with a powerful torso that suggested a weight lifter's strength. He was bullet headed with a small nose and large watery blue eyes that never seemed to blink. He had a bull frog voice. He had listened to the conversation to this point without intervening, even when his command's reputation was called into question. He returned the admiral's hard looks with equanimity. If he had been asked (out of the admiral's hearing) his opinion of that officer, he would have said: "Good combat record but not much backbone. Bends to the wind. Obviously, didn't have a good plebe year at the

Academy. Can't let him get you on the run, or he'll never let you up. Stay cool. His kind don't last very long."

"Admiral, thanks for a chance to say something on my own behalf (this with a forced smile for Anse Hughes). Let me say I think Anse did a commendable job with the court martial -- though I would have given Dell a harsher sentence. I have to contradict Anse and say there wasn't much leeway for me in what his court handed out. The recorder of the court, Lieutenant Commander Davenport, has already apologized for the oversights that led to Ensign Dell's not being ready for the court martial. But we must not expect too much from these 'Christmas Help' lawyers that Washington sends us when they feel we are not up to our responsibilities.

"As for my action on the record of the court martial...Just as Anse did, I too did my duty as I saw it. I am sure you do not mean to exert undue influence on actions that are legally mine to take. I am sure you don't expect me to heave in on your lines when you are just as or more capable of doing it with no advice or help from me. Just as Anse did with me, I have left it to you to adjust the sentence downward -- or even throw out the proceedings as you see fit. I am not emotionally involved in this matter. It is simply a matter of duty and apparently each of us interprets our duty somewhat differently.

"As for Ensign Dell's medical condition the past couple of days and his inability to answer your summons, I have directed the Commanding Officer, Marine Barracks, Pensacola to initiate an investigation as to how Ensign Dell was injured. Admiral, I will forward the results of that investigation to you as soon as I have a chance to read it."

"Great balls of fire, Felix, you should have been a lawyer. You have just fed me the biggest line of bullshit, obfuscation, and fan dancing that I have ever heard. Now I am going to tell you what I am going to do. I am ordering you to call on Ensign Dell as soon as you leave this office and to apologize for the beating -- Felix, you just try to tell me this kid wasn't beaten -- and that he has your personal guarantee that not only will nothing like that ever happen again on your air station, but that you will take every step to bring the culprits to justice. Moreover, since the medicos won't let him leave his bed to come up here, I intend to accompany you on this courtesy call and talk to him myself.

"Next, I am going to order an investigation -- Lud, write this down -- of your disciplinary and legal procedures concerning treatment of personnel being held in custody before trial and the holding of those convicted at courts martial. Lud, I want you to make the CO of the Marine Barracks a party to that investigation. Max (nodding to his chief of staff), I want you to head up that investigation.

"Max, call the hospital and tell them Felix and I are on our way over there to see Ensign Dell. Lud, you can come along to see that I don't step in any shit along the way."

Fifteen minutes later, Admiral Harding, Captain Cushing, and Captain Lud Browning were accompanied by the Commanding Officer of the Pensacola Naval Hospital as they trooped in to see Ensign Dell.

Jack was awake. His face was bruised and swollen.

He was missing a front tooth and his ribs were taped. He struggled to come to some semblance of attention when faced with his high ranking visitors. But he soon fell back on the bed with a groan. "Good afternoon sir, sirs," Jack lisped."

Admiral Harding made the introductions and said that Captain Cushing had something to say. Cushing then launched into a wooden, by rote apology that he must have mentally rehearsed on the ride over to the hospital. As he said the words, he grew crimson and near the end he was croaking. He finished with, "Is there anything more, Admiral?" making it obvious to all concerned that the apology was a matter of orders and duty, and not in any way genuine.

"No, Captain Cushing. We will finish our conversation privately in my office this afternoon."

"Now, I would like to be alone with Ensign Dell. "All of you get back to work. I have some questions for this young man."

As they filed out of Jack's room Harding faced the window away from Jack. After a moment he turned and looked Jack in the eye for about thirty seconds. Then he made up his mind to find out what was behind the evidence presented in the court martial. He was convinced the record he had reviewed did not tell the entire story.

"There is only one other Navy officer who looked me in the eye like that, and he was my son in law. Unfortunately, he is now dead. But I am not here to tell you about my misfortunes, I am here to listen to your story.

"This morning I reviewed the record of your court martial and the action of Captain Cushing on it. As you know he affirmed the findings and the sentence. My staff has recommended to me that as reviewing officer, I sign off on it as well. I want to hear from you why I shouldn't do that. I want to hear from you why you launched such a harebrained scheme. Hell, if you'd only waited two weeks, you would have seen that they had to throw the case out. No way they would retry such a case in wartime."

"Yes sir, but I didn't know that. I was scared as hell. I was being sent home in disgrace when all I wanted to do was to get into action. Well, I got into action all right -- a lot more than I bargained for. Fortunately for me, my first skipper was the best man I have ever known. He was a father and friend to me. He taught me how to shoot and how to grow up in less than five months. Most important, he taught me how to accept responsibility. You may have heard of him sir; he was Lieutenant Commander Gus Prather -- a real man and a leader.

Harding felt as though he had suffered a hammer blow. He turned to the window as he felt the tears come to his eyes. His thoughts went back to last spring when his daughter received a telegram and her sorrow and anger as she cried on his shoulder. Harding's son in law, Gus Prather, was receiving a belated eulogy from the frightened and hero worshipping junior officer lying hurt in the bed before him. This was one of Gus's boys. He probably mentioned him in his letters. He and Gus were kindred souls though Harding knew in his own heart that Gus was the better man. He was proud of his son-in-law, the way he combined professional competence with honor -- a man who would have been another Jimmie Flatley if he had lived long enough.

Getting control of himself, Harding asked, "Did Gus...er Prather know about your deception?"

"No sir, but he kept suspecting something. He didn't press me, but he knew something wasn't right. But as long as I did my job, he never pressed me for answers. We joked that we would both come clean in a Tokyo bar when it was all over. Skipper Prather never could square who I was and how I performed in combat with what was in John Deal's service and training records. It nearly killed me to deceive the man who had done so much for me and who I so admired. The Navy Crosses that John Deal won really belonged to Gus Prather."

"Son, I know Gus Prather's widow. At some point I am going to ask you to call on her and tell her what you have just told me. That is all I have for now. I will send word over later today what action I am going to take on your court martial."

As Admiral Harding went to the door, he turned and said, "Good shooting, Dell. Next time pick your targets more carefully. Good luck and good bye."

Later that afternoon, Captain Lud Browning came by to see Jack. Browning looked at him and said, "Dell, you are the luckiest SOB I know. The Admiral has suspended your sentence for two years. He has arranged with BUPERS to attach you to his staff for two years and to send you on temporary duty to Washington to straighten out John Deal's and Jack Dell's records with the

Board of Correction of Naval Records. When you finish that job, he is going to recommend to that same BCNR that you be promoted to Lieutenant and that the awards erroneously given to John Deal be given to you.

"And, oh yes, he said you are to personally express your condolences to Mr. and Mrs. Deal wherever they may be. And finally, the Admiral wants you to call on Mrs. Augustus Prather, his daughter who lives in Coronado. Do you know her?"

Two days later, Jack was found fit enough to leave the hospital. But before he checked out he was visited again by Captain Browning.

"Dell, you leave for Washington later this week, but you have one more chore before you go. The public relations folks have set you up for a press conference tomorrow morning. You are the star attraction -- the national papers and wire services will be well represented. You may not know it but you have it in your power to do the Navy a lot of good or a lot of harm. I hope you make the right choice. The Admiral has gone out on a limb for you and a lot of the old salts will be after his hide for caving in to what they perceive is pressure from the press."

"Sir, thanks for the advice. The Navy doesn't owe me anything -- and I don't owe it anything either. I intend to tell the truth about what I did wrong and how I grew up during the war. For sure, I can't tell how a bunch of reporters will interpret what I tell them. But I have no axes to grind or scores to settle. Maggie and I just want to get all that behind us. I will say that it is good to know that the

Navy system of justice works -- at least it did in my case. I got racked up real good -- but I deserved it. But it also gave me a fair shake when I was down. I'll never forget that. If there isn't anything else, sir? Maggie and my son Johnnie are waiting outside. Good morning sir."

That evening at their small house, Jack raised a glass of champagne (a beverage he had last had in San Francisco during that memorable Christmas leave in 1943) to Lieutenant Abraham Lincoln Smith.

"Here is to the best goddam ambulance chaser in the Navy -- a defender of lost causes, a paragon for shaking off undeserved insults, and a good friend. A guy who never let up. A guy who took on the system and won. A guy who if he was a fighter pilot, I would want on my wing."

Abe smiled and returned the compliment, "Any quack can look good if he has first rate material to work with! "But I want to raise a toast to your leading petty officer, "Chief" Wartburg. His buddy was the court steno and gave him a lot of good info that got fed to the newspapers. You can argue that he wasn't loyal to his CO, that bastard Cushing, but he sure was loyal to his boss Jack Dell.!"

After a moment, Jack raised his glass for another toast. "I want to thank two very special ladies: Mrs. John Deal who showed compassion and love to this worthless SOB, and to Mrs. Jack Dell who returned him to what passes for the paths of righteousness. "This lady was married to two aviators and gave her all to both."

Maggie's eyes glistened as she looked at her champagne glass. "God, Jack -- Abe --- I am so damn glad it is over. I don't have to be afraid to answer the telephone, I don't have to be afraid to open a letter, I don't have to be afraid to answer the door." She started to break down and lowered her head, her body shaken by great sobs.

Jack rose and put his arm around her and looked at Abe. "Now we have to make Mrs. John Deal an honest woman. I need your help one more time, Abe, to convince the State of California that Mrs. Deal is in fact Mrs. Dell."

"California may be tougher than the Navy, but give me a shot at it."

Maggie closed the evening by saying, "Not so fast you bastards. A lady likes to be asked before going down the aisle, particularly a widow lady. Here's to John Deal, may the bastard rest in peace and to Jack Dell -- an unlucky guy who finally got lucky and shared it with me!"

Epilogue

From the obituary column of the San Diego Union, September 17, 150.

Lieutenant Commander Jack Dell USN was killed while flying on a combat mission over North Korea on August 31st. At the time he was commanding officer of Fighter Squadron 183 flying from USS Nassau. Commander Dell was commissioned from the Aviation Cadet program in 1943 and had a distinguished wartime career in the South Pacific participating in the campaigns in the Solomons, the Marshalls, and the Mariannas. Late in the war he was stationed at NAS Pensacola and after the war attended the Navy General Line School. He subsequently served in several fighter squadrons before taking command of VF 183.

Late in World War II Lieutenant Commander Dell in a highly publicized case of mistaken identity was the subject of legal proceedings by the Navy, but was later cleared of all charges. Commander Dell received the highest decorations the nation can award. After the war he was awarded the Congressional Medal of Honor for his heroic action in shooting down eight Japanese aircraft in a single day in June 1944, and with leading an attack that destroyed an entire Japanese torpedo bomber formation attacking U.S. carrier groups. Earlier he had been awarded two Navy crosses and numerous aerial combat awards.

After World War II he was encouraged to write a book about his experiences and cooperate in the writing of a screenplay for Hollywood. But he took great pains to

Epilogue

From the obituary column of the San Diego Union, September 17, 1950.

Lieutenant Commander Jack Dell USN was killed while flying on a combat mission over North Korea on August 31st. At the time he was commanding officer of Fighter Squadron 183 flying from USS Nassau. Commander Dell was commissioned from the Aviation Cadet program in 1943 and had a distinguished wartime career in the South Pacific participating in the campaigns in the Solomons, the Marshalls, and the Mariannas. Late in the war he was stationed at NAS Pensacola and after the war attended the Navy General Line School. He subsequently served in several fighter squadrons before taking command of VF 183.

Late in World War II Lieutenant Commander Dell in a highly publicized case of mistaken identity was the subject of legal proceedings by the Navy, but was later cleared of all charges. Commander Dell received the highest decorations the nation can award. After the war he was awarded the Congressional Medal of Honor for his heroic action in shooting down eight Japanese aircraft in a single day in June 1944, and with leading an attack that destroyed an entire Japanese torpedo bomber formation attacking U.S. carrier groups. Earlier he had been awarded two Navy crosses and numerous aerial combat awards.

After World War II he was encouraged to write a book about his experiences and cooperate in the writing of a screenplay for Hollywood. But he took great pains to separate himself from his wartime exploits. Many reporters called him the 'reluctant hero.'

Lieutenant Commander Dell is survived by his wife of six years, Margaret Fitzgibbons Dell of Coronado and the couple's three sons, John Deal Dell, Augustus Prather Dell, and Abraham Smith Dell. A memorial service will be held at 10 AM Thursday at the NAS North Island base chapel. The family has asked that in lieu of flowers contributions be forwarded to the Naval Academy Alumni Association marked for the Commander Augustus Prather Memorial Fund.

Denlinger's Publishers, Ltd., "The InstaBook publisher for tomorrow's great authors... today!", hopes you have enjoyed this book.

We will forward your emailed comments to the author upon request. [support@thebookden.com].

Visit our on-line bookstore for additional **InstaBook** titles, electronic book titles **(eBooks)**, and **Rocket** edition titles. [www.thebookden.com].

This book was produced by **InstaBook**, book-on-demand, system technology.

Mission Statement
We will earnestly try to enrich and entertain our customers through reading by promoting one of our constitutional rights, "freedom of speech." And, with honesty and integrity, strive to recognize and promote authors by publishing their works.

Denlinger's Publishers & Bookstore

P.O. Box 1030 – Edgewater, FL 32132-1030